THE TRIAL OF GEORGE W. BUSH

TERRY JASTROW

SQUAREONE
PUBLISHERS

This is a work of fiction. The story is set in the future and is a product of the author's imagination. While there are real people, places, institutions, and events referenced in the story, they are portrayed in a fictional manner. The actual events, such as the Iraq War, are based on publicly available facts.

Cover Photo: International Criminal Court at The Hague, Netherlands
Cover Photo Credit: Terry Jastrow
Cover Designer: Jeannie Rosado
Typesetter: Gary A. Rosenberg

Square One Publishers
115 Herricks Road • Garden City Park, NY 11040
(516) 535-2010 • (877) 900-BOOK
www.squareonepublishers.com

Library of Congress Cataloging-in-Publication Data
Names: Jastrow, Terry, author.
Title: The trial of George W. Bush / Terry Jastrow.
Description: Garden City Park, NY : Square One Publishers, [2021] |
    Includes bibliographical references.
Identifiers: LCCN 2020031175 (print) | LCCN 2020031176 (ebook) | ISBN
    9780757005060 (paperback) | ISBN 9780757055065 (ebook)
Subjects: LCSH: International Criminal Court—Fiction. | Bush, George W.
    (George Walker), 1946—Fiction. | Iraq War, 2003-2011—Fiction. | War
    crime trials—Fiction. | GSAFD: Legal stories.
Classification: LCC PS3610.A87 T74 2021 (print) | LCC PS3610.A87 (ebook)
    | DDC 813/.6—dc23
LC record available at https://lccn.loc.gov/2020031175
LC ebook record available at https://lccn.loc.gov/2020031176

Printed in the United States of America

10   9   8   7   6   5   4   3   2   1

Contents

To the many men and women from many countries
who died or were wounded in the Iraq War.

Acknowledgments

I would like to express my thanks to many people who helped inform and guide this narrative. Much appreciation goes to William Schabas for making the Mount Everest of international law seem climbable with his excellent book *An Introduction to the International Criminal Court*.

I would like to thank my many international criminal law experts in both Europe and the United States for their patient, educational, and useful assistance. I would mention their names, but all preferred that I didn't.

Special thanks go out to international law expert Mike Kelly. If I were to take a course on international criminal law, he would be the person I would most like to have as my professor.

I would like to thank my wonderful collection of assistants, editors, and proofreaders for their able assistance. If this book is a good read, they helped make it so. I would also like to thank my longtime friend, attorney, and golfing partner, Barry Hirsch, who has never wavered in his belief in me, or in his support of my art.

Last but certainly not least, I would like to thank my wife, Anne Archer, for a million reasons and counting, beginning with her saying yes to the most important question I ever asked.

Preface

In his Gettysburg Address, Abraham Lincoln pleaded that America represent "a new birth of freedom . . . and that government of the people, by the people, for the people, shall not perish from the Earth." Sadly, Lincoln's beloved America is perishing. Unlike at any other time in history, Americans are confused, conflicted, contentious, troubled, and fearful. What is happening today, if left unchallenged and unchecked, is a disaster in the making that could destroy much if not all of what is considered great about America.

The inevitable fact about this fictional story is that nobody knows if it will become a reality or not. Among the great things about freedom of thought and expression in the United States, however, is that they are baked into its DNA, and have been since its outset. The existential question is: Will such freedoms exist in the future?

Before continuing, I would like to disclose a few things that may influence your reading or opinion of this story. My mother's father was a descendant of America's 2nd and 6th presidents, John Adams and John Quincy Adams, respectively, and a family that arrived on the *Mayflower* in 1620. I was born in Denver and raised in Colorado, Oklahoma, and Texas. I'm as "American pie" as they come.

While I was growing up in Midland, Texas, my family knew George H. W. Bush's family. In fact, I played Little League Baseball against George W. Bush, and while I'm too modest to mention who won, George's team lost. During my time at the University of Houston in the late 1960s, George was a young oilman living in the same city. We saw each other socially, as we were dating twin sisters, Susie and Beth. When George was governor of Texas, my wife and I visited him at the state capitol, where he told us, with his cowboy boots propped up on his desk, that he was running for president because Colin Powell wouldn't. George is a fun guy, loves to laugh, and is full of great stories, but over time it has become clear that he and I have very different views on war and peace.

Admittedly, the chance of what you're about to read becoming a reality is slim, but if one could know how much longer George W. Bush will live, who will be elected president of the United States during the remainder of his life, if Democrats or Republicans will control the US Congress, if the United States will rejoin the International Criminal Court, and who the ICC prosecutors will be during the remainder of Mr. Bush's life, then one would be able to make an informed guess. One thing, however, is sad but true: If the leadership of a country is left unchecked and unchallenged by its citizenry, then the opportunity for calamity and the possibility of criminal activity will exist and persist.

Introduction

In the wake of World War II, smart men and woman from many nations created the United Nations, which is located today in New York City. In June 1998, under the auspices of the UN, legal experts from around the world gathered in Rome to discuss, debate, and finally draft the Rome Statute of the International Criminal Court, which established genocide, crimes against humanity, war crimes, and the crime of aggression as core international crimes and created the International Criminal Court. The International Criminal Court is meant for those occasions when countries are unable or unwilling to bring perpetrators of these core crimes to justice themselves. Its official seat is located in The Hague, Netherlands. The Rome Statute went into force on July 1, 2002, having reached sixty signatories, the minimum number required for it to enter into force.

Today, there are one hundred ninety-five countries in the world, one hundred and twenty-three of which are parties to the Rome Statute of the International Criminal Court, meaning these countries have not only signed the statute but also ratified or acceded to it. Why, you may ask, aren't more countries parties to this important statute, such as the United States? Well, powerful people in non-party countries do not want to be governed by international law because they know they are committing crimes under international law or may do so in the future, and thus would be subject to arrest and trial for these crimes at the International Criminal Court.

In 2003, yet another destructive and perhaps illegal war occurred, the Iraq War, which resulted in the deaths of thousands of coalition soldiers, including 4,424 US soldiers, and hundreds of thousands of Iraqis.

The following story is set in the future and is a product of the author's imagination. While the information relating to the Iraq War is factual, the real people, places, and institutions that appear in the narrative have been fictionalized.

The president of the United States, with his contrarian personality and disquieting policies and practices, has created a dystopian state. He has withdrawn America from protective treaties with close allies, pulled US troops out of allied countries, negotiated trade agreements with rogue nations, done everything in his power to insulate Americans from the legal liability set forth by international law, and imposed sanctions on individuals with close ties to the International Criminal Court. It is in this contentious state of affairs that our story begins.

Calculating that bringing a former US president to trial would be more feasible than a sitting or recently retired president, the ICC conducts an investigation of George W. Bush in connection with crimes that may have been committed during the Iraq War. It concludes that the 43rd president of the United States should be brought to trial. Whether or not this fictional story becomes fact is up to brave citizens who can no longer tolerate innocent people being victimized by needless wars, and who insist upon the application of established laws to bring those responsible for the victimization to justice.

1

Welcome to the International Criminal Court

*"Violence is immoral because it thrives on hatred
rather than love. It destroys community and makes
brotherhood impossible. It leaves society in monologue
rather than dialogue. Violence ends up defeating itself."*

—MARTIN LUTHER KING JR.

EARLY ON A GLORIOUS SEPTEMBER MORNING in St. Andrews, Scotland, former President of the United States George W. Bush approached the first tee of the world's most famous golf course to play a round of golf he would not finish. Assembled around the first tee were a few hundred local residents and a handful of members of the Royal & Ancient Golf Club. Known simply as the R&A, the club is the governing body and custodian of the rules in all golfing countries except the United States, which has its own governing body.

Precisely at 8:00 AM, George W. Bush and two club members approached the first tee and were greeted by R&A Secretary Harold Maxwell.

"Gentlemen. Good day to all," Maxwell said.

"It'll be a good day if I don't chunk it into the Swilcan Burn on the first hole," Bush said, shaking hands with the secretary, "or yank it into the Road Bunker at seventeen."

"I'm sure you'll do just fine."

"You're more sure than I am."

Secretary Maxwell chuckled. "We were very pleased to welcome your father, George H. W. Bush, here as a new member after he had finished his presidency."

"Yeah, he loved golf, and he loved St. Andrews, that's for sure."

"There's a little-known story about your father that says a lot about him as a human being," Maxwell continued. "In December of the year he played his first round on the Old Course, he sent his caddie a handwritten letter thanking him for making his experience at St. Andrews so special and wishing him a Merry Christmas. I do believe that was a first."

"He must've been a good caddie."

"Must have been."

"Guessing you fellows don't allow mulligans here," Bush said, looking out at the first fairway.

"No mulligans here, but we can offer a swallow of Scotch whiskey if that'll settle your nerves."

"Not my nerves I got a problem with; it's my damn golf swing. Forsakes me every time when I need it the most . . . like now!"

It would be fair to say that every golfer in the world dreams of playing the Old Course at St. Andrews. George Bush Jr. approached the ball, took his stance, nervously jerked the club away, and swung. Mercifully, the ball curved only slightly to the right and came to rest on the fairway. Bush smiled mischievously.

"Not too bad for a broken-down old president. What's the course record around here, anyway?"

"In the Open Championship, sixty-three," Secretary Maxwell answered, raising an eyebrow.

"Sixty-three? Hell, I will've hit it that many times by the twelfth hole," Bush said as he winked at the secretary and stepped aside to allow his playing partners to tee off.

From a position two hundred yards away on a public footpath that bordered the fairway, a middle-aged man lowered his binoculars and turned to saunter away, whistling as he went. As he reached up to scratch his nose, he spoke quietly into a microphone buried inside the sleeve of his sweater.

"Target on time and in position."

In a secluded wooded area one mile from the golf course, a nondescript brown van and midsize blue car were parked side by side. Sitting inside the van were ten highly trained UN Special Forces commandos, who had been selected from the world's best militaries to support the activity of the World Court. Each was holding an assortment of weaponry. Inside the car sat Lawrence Archer, a deputy prosecutor at the International Criminal Court, and two more UN commandos. Hearing the description of George Bush's wardrobe, Archer keyed his radio and responded, "Copy that. How many Secret Service?"

"Four," the spy answered, looking through his binoculars again to confirm. "Easy to spot, definitely American, big, fit, wearing earpieces, walking in the fairway close by the target, you can't miss 'em."

"Copy that, thanks," Archer spoke into his radio. "Okay everybody, Cowboy Justice is a go."

The pilots sitting in the cockpits of a Hawker 800XP and a Learjet 85, both with engines idling on a secured runway at Rotterdam The Hague Airport, received the message and answered back in turn.

"Cowboy Justice is a go. Hawker 1, copy that."

"Learjet1, copy that as well."

With that confirmation, the drivers of the van and the car exchanged informal salutes, started their vehicles, and headed inconspicuously to their preplanned location next to the seventeenth fairway of the Old Course. The Hawker took off in an angry roar from the airport, followed quickly by the Learjet.

The most famous hole on the Old Course at St. Andrews is the seventeenth, commonly referred to as the Road Hole. The green sits hard by a cobblestone road bordered by a stone wall, which for centuries has presented unusual and difficult challenges for golfers. George W. Bush, midway through a Cuban cigar, arrived at the seventeenth tee along with his playing partners and the caddies. Bush put his cigar aside and considered his options as his caddie, Oliver Croft, offered a word of encouragement.

"Nice and easy does it, sir," Croft said.

"Nice and easy is not my strong suit, but I'll try," Bush said before slicing his tee shot into the right rough and providing his own commentary. "More or less like Jack Nicklaus did it."

"More 'less' than 'more,' sir, I'm afraid," Croft responded with a wink.

Bush winked back, put his cigar back into his mouth, and headed down the fairway, saying, "Let's go see if we can birdie this bad boy."

Simultaneously with Bush's tee shot, the brown van and blue car pulled into the parking lot of the Jigger Inn, a famous watering hole located to the right of the seventeenth fairway. As the vehicles pulled to a stop, UN Special Forces inside readied their weaponry in compliance with carefully scripted orders.

As Bush approached his ball on the seventeenth fairway and his Secret Service agents began to create a ten-foot perimeter around him, the UN commandos rushed onto the fairway, firing tranquilizer rounds at the agents, who suddenly dropped to the ground, incapacitated and in a state of semi-consciousness. Seeing his Secret Service protection lying immobile on the ground and realizing he could do nothing, George W. Bush turned to his playing partners and said, "Stay calm. Don't say anything, don't move, and don't try to be a hero. They're here for me."

Lawrence Archer approached the former president and handed him an arrest warrant.

"Mr. George W. Bush, I am Lawrence Archer, deputy prosecutor of the International Criminal Court. I hereby serve you with this arrest warrant and place you under arrest for immediate conveyance to the ICC in The Hague to stand trial for crimes against humanity and war crimes of which you are accused. Upon arrival at the ICC you will have ample opportunity to communicate with your country's government and with legal counsel of your choice. You will not be harmed if you do not resist."

"I don't care who you are or where you're from, but I do know you are in deep shit for doing this," Bush said, ripping up the arrest warrant and flinging it back in the deputy prosecutor's face.

Ignoring the threat, Archer nodded at the UN commandos, who quickly slipped a black felt hood over Bush's head and escorted him unceremoniously off the golf course and into the van, which immediately sped away. The stealth abduction of a former president of the United States from the world's most famous golf course against his will in less than eight minutes was in stark contrast to the serene peace and quiet of the ancient town of St. Andrews, Scotland, the resting place of Saint Andrew the Apostle.

Six miles from St. Andrews, in the hamlet of Leuchars, the Hawker and Learjet landed at an RAF airfield. With clockwork precision, the van carrying Bush pulled up alongside the Learjet and four UN commandos transferred the former president to the plane. Simultaneously, other commandos secretly escorted a man who looked remarkably like George W. Bush—about the same age, height, weight, facial features, and hair color, and wearing the same clothes—onto the Hawker. Inside the jet, the commandos sat the Bush look-a-like in a window seat, and two minutes later the Hawker sped down the runway and lifted off, headed west to Glasgow. Seconds later, the Learjet carrying the real George W. Bush took off in a southeasterly direction, destination unknown.

Inside the R&A clubhouse, the secretary was on the phone with Scotland Yard, explaining what happened as best he could. Behind the eighteenth green of the Old Course, Scottish police were questioning Bush's playing partners and the caddies. What they knew would fill a thimble. What they didn't know would fill a novel.

In the sky over Scotland, two RAF jets flew up to and then alongside the Hawker. The pilots spotted a man they thought was George W. Bush, radioed that they had found the former president, and requested a convoy of military aircraft to help escort the Hawker to Glasgow. Headed in the opposite direction, the Learjet carrying George W. Bush flew close to the ground to avoid conventional radar. Aboard the plane, UN commandos removed the hood from Bush, who immediately assessed the situation and protested, "Who the hell are you guys?"

"You will understand soon enough, Mr. Bush," the attending commando responded. "You do not need to worry. You will not be harmed."

"You're British, aren't you?"

"Yes."

"Then what the hell are you doing?" Bush erupted in anger. "You're supposed to be our friend."

"No, Tony Blair is your friend," the commando shot back. "Most people hated your war."

Minutes later, the Learjet landed at its destination, Rotterdam The Hague Airport, and taxied to a stop next to a waiting chopper, the rotary blades of which were already spinning. UN security forces quickly and silently escorted Mr. Bush off the jet and into the chopper, which took off immediately.

At the same time, the Hawker, now boxed in by four escort jets flying in close proximity, was forced to land at Glasgow Airport and taxi to a stop. Police cars with red lights spinning and sirens screaming quickly circled the plane to create a three hundred and sixty-degree barricade. A dozen Scottish police officers under the command of Chief Constable Angus Duff aimed their weapons at the plane while government officials positioned themselves behind the police cars for protection. The door opened and the pilot descended the stairs, yelling in protest.

"What the hell is going on here?" he said.

"Where is he?" Chief Constable Duff responded over a megaphone from behind the barricade.

"Where is who?" the pilot answered with noted anger.

"You know who. Deliver him unharmed or you will be spending the rest of your life in a cold, dark box."

"Are you out of your mind? Your jets flew dangerously close to my aircraft in blatant violation of international flight regulations, and now you're falsely accusing me of having some mythical passenger onboard!"

Without responding, Chief Constable Duff signaled a dozen Scottish police wearing body armor and carrying machine guns to board and search the plane. A few minutes later, one of the Scottish police officers appeared at the exit door.

"Sir, George W. Bush is definitely not on this aircraft," the officer reported.

"What do you mean?" Chief Constable Duff snapped back.

"I'm not sure how I could say it any differently, sir," the officer replied, glancing at his colleagues.

Being first to report important breaking news is the most coveted prize amongst news agencies, and on this occasion it went to the British Broadcasting Company. Standing in front of a camera, microphone in hand and exuding an aura of authority earned over many years on the job, multi-award-winning journalist Elizabeth Reynolds began her report.

"This is Elizabeth Reynolds reporting from BBC News headquarters in London with a development of huge international importance. We have just learned that, earlier today, former President of the United States George W. Bush was abducted while golfing in St. Andrews, Scotland. At this time, there are more questions than answers.

"We know that Mr. Bush and two members of the Royal and Ancient Golf Club, commonly referred to as the R&A, teed off this morning on the Old Course at 8:00 AM BST. Three hours later, at approximately 11:00 AM, four middle-aged Caucasian men abducted Mr. Bush off the seventeenth fairway. According to our sources, Mr. Bush was placed in the back of a van, which immediately drove away. Mr. Bush's playing partners abandoned their game and ran straight up the eighteenth fairway to the R&A clubhouse to report the strange and troubling developments.

"Who are these people that whisked Mr. Bush off the famous golf course in Scotland? Where was Mr. Bush's Secret Service protection? If former US President Bush has been abducted from a golf course in Scotland, the international importance of the event cannot be overstated, and it presents a myriad of unwelcome questions: Who is responsible for this act of monumental hubris? Will other countries be compelled to beef up security for their former leaders traveling abroad? Where in the world is George W. Bush, and is he alive and well? Stay tuned for continuing coverage."

The peace and quiet of a sleepy summer afternoon was shattered by the sound of a helicopter landing at the International Criminal Court in The Hague, a city on the western coast of the Netherlands. As the chopper's blades continued rotating, UN security guards escorted an angry George W. Bush off the aircraft and into the reception area of the ICC Detention Centre. The walls of the smallish but functional room were bare except for a framed copy of the Rome Statute and a portrait of the UN Secretary-General. The guards led the 43rd president of the United States to a desk, where sat ICC guard Mobwana Mochella of Kenya.

"Hello, Mr. Bush," she began. "Welcome to the International Criminal Court."

"I need a private room with a secure phone that I can use to call the United States," Bush replied.

"Yes, you do, Mr. Bush," Mochella responded compassionately, "and we will ensure that happens as quickly as permitted, but first we need to complete the admission process." She pushed forward without allowing him any time to object. "Consistent with ICC protocol, I will inform you of your living quarters for the foreseeable future. Each detainee is assigned a private cell that includes a single bed, desk, chair, bookshelves, toilet, hand basin, television, and computer. We provide three meals a day, but detainees also have access to a communal kitchen if they wish to cook for themselves.

The ICC provides a variety of recreational opportunities at selected times, including walks in the courtyard, a basketball court, and an exercise gym. You can elect to partake in manual pursuits such as gardening, painting—we hear you like to paint, so that might be of interest—woodcrafts, or other such activities. You will receive medical and dental care as needed. Detainees can have visitors at prearranged times and certain phone calls are permitted; however, you should know that all calls and computer usage will be monitored."

Her welcome speech successfully delivered, Mochella reached into a nearby closet and brought out a bundle. "Here are your ICC-approved clothes and pajamas, Mr. Bush," Mochella said. "Let us know if they don't fit to your liking or you need anything else."

"Is there a Bible in the room?"

"I'll make sure there is."

"And someone will let me know when I can use a secured phone?"

"Yes, sir. That is a promise."

Now that orientation had ended, Mochella nodded at the prison guards, who escorted a tired and emotional former President George W. Bush to his prison cell. Once inside and alone, he sat on the single bed, looked around the sparsely furnished room that would be his home for the foreseeable future, and buried his face in his hands.

News of the abduction of former President George W. Bush sent America's top political, legal, and military elite into a tailspin. Not since the 9/11 attacks had so many high-powered meetings been so hastily assembled to discuss such a daunting crisis of international importance. Across the Potomac from Washington, DC, in a secure room in the Pentagon, the day culminated with a late-night strategy session that included Secretary of Defense John Cox and the Joint Chiefs of Staff, representing the Army, Marine Corps, Navy, and Air Force. Secretary Cox entered the meeting room talking.

"Gentlemen, I just got off the phone with the president and he asked for recommendations within the hour regarding the rescue of George Bush from the ICC. And then, what should we do to those responsible?"

"Sir, we already have several scenarios ready to engage," General of the Army T. D. Masterson replied.

"I hope so," Secretary Cox said, taking his seat at the head of the table. "Bombs away."

"Option one," General of the Marine Corps Thomas Shackelford began, "is to send in the SEALs from Task Force 64 currently assigned to the 6th Fleet headquartered in Naples. They can fly over the Swiss Alps and be on the ground in The Hague at eighteen hundred hours Zulu time. Minimal collateral damage expected."

"Option two," Navy Fleet Admiral Anderson Harrington stated, "is an amphibious assault. The ICC Detention Centre is two miles inland from the North Sea, easily accessible by Marine forces. The Dutch would not contest a rescue attempt, as their defenses in the area are slight and they would not be expecting an amphibious strike."

"Option three," Air Force General Barry Bledsoe added, "is a stealth Delta Force chopper landing under cover of night. Special Ops forces would breach the Detention Centre and extract former President Bush. This option utilizes ground forces and air assets already stationed in Germany; however, a higher degree of collateral damage is expected with this option."

Navy Admiral David Dorling cautioned, "Gentlemen, I understand this is a precarious situation, but if we were to recommend invading the Netherlands, a member of the United Nations and signatory of the International Criminal Court, we would be recommending military aggression that would be in contradiction to the UN Charter and committing international crimes ourselves."

The events of the day were newsworthy by anybody's definition, and the biggest and best news organizations in the United States were in an all-hands-on-deck, man-the-battle-stations frenzy. The most respected broadcasters canceled whatever programming had been scheduled to make way for nonstop reporting of the only story anybody in America cared about. Not only would ratings spike to all-time highs but also awards for outstanding news reporting would be on the line, and nobody in the biz wanted to miss out on this once-in-a-lifetime shot at greatness.

CBS's Kenneth McLane reported, "We've just learned that less than an hour ago, at approximately 11:15 AM BST, 6:15 AM EDT, former President of the United States George W. Bush was escorted from the world-famous Old Course in St. Andrews, Scotland, by unidentified commandos posing as UN security guards."

Jessica Evans stated on ABC, "Sources tell us that Mr. Bush did have the standard allotment of Secret Service agents on site, but obviously they did not provide the requisite protection needed for a former president in a foreign land. No doubt that current protocol will be the subject of much deliberation, after which, presumably, a few heads will roll."

NBC's William Huff offered, "It is believed that Mr. Bush does not travel outside the United States, as he is thought to be in some legal jeopardy in connection with waging the Iraq War, the fear being that he could be arrested and transported to the International Criminal Court in The Hague to face charges for war crimes. But any speculation in that regard would be just that, speculation."

14

On Fox News, Sarah Nichols concluded, "Mr. Bush's three playing partners and their caddies were not harmed and are reportedly cooperating with local and international law enforcement authorities. So we can only deduce that former President Bush was specifically targeted for the abduction. No doubt the perpetrators of this brazen act will eventually be found and made to pay a hefty price for this crime of international significance."

After learning about the day's events, members of the international press rushed to the International Criminal Court in The Hague like hyenas chasing a wounded animal. First to arrive at The Hague were British teams from the BBC, Sky TV, and ITV. Not long after, media giants from Europe, Russia, the United States, and elsewhere around the world arrived, including, notably, Iraq. Eventually forty-four of the world's elite news organizations began setting up shop in a park across from the ICC building with giddy anticipation of what was to come, similar to that which accompanies a presidential election, coronation of a Queen, or assassination of a world leader.

In a cell in the ICC Detention Centre, George W. Bush, wearing prison-issued pajamas, sat slumped on the edge of his bed, chastising himself for venturing outside the United States and not bothering to pay more attention to international criminal laws or the International Criminal Court.

2
Opening Volleys

*"Justice will not be served until those who are
unaffected are as outraged as those who are."*

—BENJAMIN FRANKLIN

THE INTERNATIONAL CRIMINAL COURT HAS EIGHTEEN JUDGES in residence of mixed nationality, gender, and race. In international law there are no juries, each case is assigned either one or three judges, and verdicts are rendered accordingly, by the vote of one judge or the majority vote of three judges. In the trial of George W. Bush, three judges were assigned.

Once assigned to a case, judges work to resolve all procedural matters leading up to the trial, most especially to oversee the Office of the Prosecutor as it carries out its duties to guarantee the rights of the victims and the accused, along with suspects and witnesses in a fair and honest trial. The person overseeing the trial is the chief prosecutor, whose principle function is to assign the prosecuting attorneys most suited to each case. It was not of much surprise that one of the attorneys selected to lead the prosecution in the case against George W. Bush was Michael David McBride, a hard-charging lawyer with top-of-the-class intelligence and an infectious personality.

Michael was born forty-four years earlier in Denver, Colorado, to parents who were also litigators. His mother specialized in child endangerment, prostitution, and abandonment cases. His father's beat was corporate law—specifically, corrupt banking claims of fifty million dollars or more. Michael was an outstanding high school basketball player and student body president, became a Rhodes scholar, graduated with honors from Harvard Law, and earned a scholarship to study international law at Oxford. After completing his formal education, Michael moved to London to set up a private practice specializing in international criminal law. Once there, he reconnected with a childhood girlfriend, Cheryl Stapleford, and soon thereafter they were married. When the ICC recruited him to be a prosecuting attorney, Michael quickly accepted, packed his bags, and moved to The Hague, leaving Cheryl in London to fend for herself.

Michael McBride was selected as one of the prosecutors in the trial of George W. Bush specifically because he was an American. To have a German or an Italian prosecuting a former US president would play into a defense argument regarding the legitimacy of the Court and the audacity of sitting in judgment of decisions made by an American president.

Co–prosecuting attorney Nadia Shadid was born thirty-nine years earlier and raised in Fallujah, Iraq, by a father who was a schoolteacher and mother who was a well-known and much-respected leader in establishing fundamental human rights for Muslim women. Although Nadia's family was Sunni, she grew up with an assortment of Shiite, Kurdish, and Christian friends. While studying law at the University of Baghdad, she dated a fellow student who worked at night as a drummer in a local band. According to friends who knew them well, their dreams took divergent paths when Nadia discovered she was happier alone than with a man she did not totally love.

During her youth, Nadia's family lived next door to Ibrahim Yasin, one of Iraq's most respected attorneys specializing in international law. Upon graduating from university, Mr. Yasin invited Nadia to join his prestigious London firm, Alliss, Blankenship & Coe. After six formative years during which she worked in the international litigation division, Nadia applied for and got an entry position in the Office of the Prosecutor at the International Criminal Court in The Hague.

Nadia and Michael had worked together on several cases and had developed a mutual admiration and fondness. They were two very different people from very different worlds who found a common passion in international criminal law. Now they would bear the honor and burden of prosecuting a case against a former president of the United States. In the late afternoon of a long day of preparation, Michael and Nadia went for an afternoon walk in a park near the ICC. Along the way, Michael challenged his colleague.

"In order to prosecute this case effectively, wouldn't it be useful to understand the point of view of the Iraqi people about the Iraq War?" Michael asked.

"My people are conflicted," Nadia replied without hesitation. "How one thinks of such things is influenced by one's religious affiliation: Sunni, Shiite, Kurd, Christian, or whatever. If you are Sunni, as Saddam was, you might be upset that he was forcibly removed from power. If you are Shiite, Kurd, or Christian, you're probably happy to no longer be living under his rule."

Michael pressed for more. "One would think it would simply be a question of the common good for the greatest number of Iraqi citizens," he said. "Sooner or later, it would seem, there needs to be a common ground of understanding that the majority of Iraqi people could agree upon for the safety and security of all."

"Spoken like a true Westerner," Nadia said with a hint of a smile. "The fundamental differences can be traced back thousands of years, and they are not simple or easy to overcome."

"I understand, but take America, there are significant differences in the culture . . . rich/poor, religious/atheist, black/white, Democrat/Republican . . . but in desperate times, Americans pull together as Americans. They seem to put their differences aside with the understanding they will ultimately be stronger together than divided."

"A theoretical deduction of which you might have a hard time convincing some Americans."

"Maybe so," Michael said and pivoted to another question. "Do you think the majority of Iraqis are happy we're bringing Bush to trial?"

"Some are, not all. Many Iraqis opposed the war and will be happy to see those who caused it face justice—starting with George W. Bush."

Michael thought it might be useful to provide some perspective. "You are, of course, aware that George W. Bush didn't receive the majority of votes in his presidential election against Al Gore in 2000?"

"I am," Nadia said.

"He won after a highly contentious recount in the state of Florida, where his brother Jeb was governor. Bush actually got five hundred and forty-something thousand fewer votes than Gore."

"And how a democracy could have allowed that to happen still shocks me."

"Yes, we can thank our Electoral College for that, sad but true."

"And stupid. Can't anything be done about it?"

"Well, the idea of abolishing the Electoral College in America comes up every few years, but so far political chicanery has won out over common sense."

As the Earth turned away from the sun, leaving a magnificent sunset of pinks and purples, they paused to take in the grandeur of the western sky. After a moment of reflection, Nadia said in a voice barely loud enough to hear, "Michael, if we don't win this case after what George Bush did to my people, I will take a slow walk into that sea."

Michael was surprised and touched. "I understand, but it's not considered best practice for prosecuting attorneys to let their personal passions interfere with the administration of justice."

She paused for a moment before speaking. "Michael, can I share something with you, and ask that it be kept confidential between us?"

"Sure."

"My favorite uncle, my father's oldest brother, Jamaal, was killed three days into the Iraq War, in Baghdad, in a firefight with American soldiers." Nadia looked away to collect herself. "Sometimes, at night, when I'm alone with my thoughts, I think about him because I hate how cruel war is to those who are made to fight it."

On the morning of the pretrial hearing, UN guards, prosecution and defense attorneys, and all manner of Court personnel were in their appointed seats. George W. Bush, wearing the same golf clothes he had on the day before in St. Andrews, sat in the accused's chair. At 9:00 AM CEST, per protocol, the clerk stood and announced, "The International Criminal Court is now in session. All rise." All did except George Bush.

The honorable and highly esteemed Judge Harrison Hurst-Brown of Great Britain, wearing an ankle-length navy blue robe accentuated by purple stripes running from shoulder to foot, walked briskly to his seat at the judges' table and sat, as did all others in the courtroom. Hurst-Brown looked around the courtroom to ensure all was in order, and then began with a noticeable hint of gravity.

"Good day, everybody. Welcome to the International Criminal Court."

Bush, refusing to acknowledge him, looked away and said nothing.

"When the ICC was created," Hurst-Brown continued, "it provided for three categories of international crimes to be investigated and prosecuted as and when necessary: genocide, crimes against humanity, and war crimes. George W. Bush, you are here to stand trial for war crimes in connection with the Iraq War, March 2003 through December 2011. The ICC has very strict protocol regarding the administration of justice.

"The question of jurisdiction is the first and fundamental question of every case in international law. It is true, unfortunately, that the United States is not a member of the ICC. However, the Rome Statute provides that a nonmember state, such as Iraq, may, by submitting a formal request to the Registrar, accept the jurisdiction of the Court. The sovereign state of Iraq has lodged such a declaration, and the ICC has accepted jurisdiction in connection with crimes that the defendant may or may not have been committed during the Iraq War."

Then Hurst-Brown looked directly at the defendant. "According to the Pre-Trial Chamber's findings, the ICC is satisfied that the crimes with which you, George W. Bush, are charged, have been correctly brought within the jurisdiction of this Court. It is a fundamental pillar of international criminal law that every person is entitled to select his or her own legal counsel, commonly referred to as the defense. At this point in the proceeding, Mr. Bush, you have a choice. You can elect to defend yourself, commonly referred to as self-representation, or be represented by your chosen legal counsel. Should you choose the latter, we will suspend any further activity until such time as your team has arrived and you have had ample opportunity to consult with them. Would you like to make that determination now, or be accorded the time to consider the question?"

Bush sat stoically, saying nothing.

"Mr. Bush, will you select a defense team or self-represent? Or do you require more time to think about it?"

The former president of the United States stared at the ICC judge for a long moment before answering.

"I've considered the question and here's my answer: This is bullshit. I am fully aware of the ICC and its pluses and minuses. I was the president of the United States for two terms and performed my solemn duty to protect and defend my country in a manner entirely appropriate under the circumstances at the time, regardless of what you may think or say."

Refusing to acknowledge Bush's taunt, Hurst-Brown continued with his business.

"Following the end of the Iraq War in December 2011, additional information has been found that influences the prosecution's opinion of the war as it relates to the commission of war crimes and possibly other crimes. Now, Mr. Bush, what will it be: self-represent or select a defense team?"

"I'm a citizen of the United States of America, and, as such, not subject to ICC investigation or prosecution. My actions were well known by the American people, the US Congress, and the US Supreme Court, all of which concurred that my decisions during the Iraq War, including the removal of one of the most evil dictators the world has ever known, were not only justifiable, but necessary. My answer is that I will not stand for this absurd, unjustified, and probably illegal trial proposed by the ICC. My activities as president of the United States relative to the Iraq War were performed in accordance with United States law, the law of the land. I'm not some outlaw gunslinger you can bring in here for a lynch mob hanging. Be careful how you respond, Mr. Judge, because you yourself will be held accountable by international legal authorities for your actions."

"My name, Mr. Bush, is Harrison Hurst-Brown," the judge countered with growing impatience. "The International Criminal Court is comprised of member states representing the majority of the peoples of the world. It has a specifically prescribed due process of law that we will follow whether you approve of it or not. Now, as you have declined your right to assemble a defense team, it leaves you to defend yourself, and so we will proceed accordingly. The Court will now inform you of your rights."

Left with no other apparent option, Bush stood.

"Under great protest and with the admission of nothing, you leave me no choice other than to assemble a defense team."

That said, Hurst-Brown rapped his gavel and announced, "The Court will recess until Mr. Bush's defense team has arrived and had appropriate time to confer." Rapping his gavel a final time, he concluded the day's session. "The Prosecutor v. George W. Bush is adjourned until further notice."

On days such as this one, there is so much content that news organizations have to scramble to gather and report it all coherently. The BBC's Elizabeth Reynolds, dressed in a perfectly tailored black suit, began her report.

"It was a historic day in international criminal law, as for the first time the former leader of a superpower has been brought to the International Criminal Court to face criminal charges. This was a day that many legal pundits thought would never come, and some historical perspective might be useful to understand the gravity of the occasion. Joining me now is Sir Nigel Pemberton, a renowned

British solicitor and friend to the friendless in London's criminal justice system. Sir Nigel, what is the overarching significance of this move by the ICC to try a former president of the United States?"

"My goodness, Elizabeth, the significance cannot be overstated. Following the horrible world wars of the twentieth century, peace-loving peoples from around the world began to advocate forcefully for the creation of international criminal law, which would ultimately stand above, and have force over, national courts. The United Nations General Assembly held a five-week diplomatic conference in June of 1998 to come up with a convention on the establishment of an international criminal court, which yielded a treaty called the Rome Statute. One hundred and twenty countries voted to adopt the treaty, seven countries voted against its adoption, and twenty-one countries abstained. Once sixty of the signatory countries had ratified the treaty, the Rome Statute finally entered into force in July 2002. The stage was set for the creation of the first International Criminal Court. During initial negotiations, the United States made a few helpful contributions, but in the end it was apparently unhappy with the scope of power accorded to the ICC and did not join."

Elizabeth sought clarification. "And many around the world understood this to mean the United States simply did not want its citizens to be subject to international legal jurisdiction?"

"Yes, but over time, America softened its opposition to the ICC, and at the end of his presidency, Bill Clinton signed the Rome Statute, although he did not submit it to the US Senate for ratification. Immediately upon taking office, George W. Bush approached the UN to see if the Clinton signature could be revoked. While international law does not permit a treaty to be unsigned, the Vienna Convention does allow for a country to change its mind after signature. Accordingly, Mr. Bush's legal eagles quickly withdrew

America's signature via a diplomatic note to the UN, declaring, 'in connection with the Rome Statute of the International Criminal Court, the United States does not intend to become a party to the treaty.' Regrettably, this stance taken by Mr. Bush as president of the United States has not changed, but he, like all people, is a citizen of the world, and, as such, must be held accountable by international law."

"How could he *not* be?" Elizabeth questioned. "The ICC has tried many cases over the years with notable success, such as the sentencing of Radovan Karadžić to prison for ethnic cleansing in the former Yugoslavia and the slaughter of eight thousand Muslims in Srebrenica."

"Correct, but none are of more import than this case against a former US president. Until now, only heads or former heads of minor states have faced international law: Radovan Karadžić, Charles Taylor of Liberia, Slobodan Milošević of Serbia, Omar al-Bashir of Sudan, and others—all relatively minor characters in small countries. The United States, however, is the most super of superpowers."

"And so, the ICC commenced the trial of George W. Bush with the anticipation it would set a precedent of trying leaders or former leaders of the world's most powerful countries in the future as and when warranted."

"Yes, and let's not forget, Elizabeth, that while George W. Bush had many co-conspirators in the Iraq War, including Vice President Dick Cheney, Secretary of Defense Donald Rumsfeld, and British Prime Minister Tony Blair, international law requires that the single person most responsible for the crime or crimes be tried first."

"Starting with George W. Bush," Elizabeth said, finishing Sir Nigel's thought.

"Yes, with others to follow as warranted in due course," Sir Nigel said, nodding in agreement.

Elizabeth concluded the interview with appropriate gravity. "Thank you, Sir Nigel. It sounds like the legitimacy and longevity of the International Criminal Court could be on trial along with George W. Bush."

Even with the monumental responsibility the ICC has to uphold the rule of law on an international scale, it does not have a dedicated military force to protect and defend itself. It must rely on armed forces provided by various ICC member countries and a variety of local forces in The Hague. And so it was that the ICC had to deal with an attack by an angry nation, an angry superpower no less, the United States of America.

After gathering at the USAG Wiesbaden Army base near Frankfurt, Germany, a team of twenty finely trained and well-equipped Special Operations Forces under the command of US Marine Captain Richard Rattigan boarded four Bell UH-1Y Venom helicopters and headed for the ICC with the urgent intent of extracting former President George W. Bush.

Following landings on the rocky beaches of the North Sea, the SOF team deplaned under the cover of night, spread out, and traversed the two-kilometer journey to the ICC Detention Centre. Very much aware of the invasion, a well-trained, well-armed permanent UN security force inside the ICC Detention Centre manned its battle stations to repel the attack. Four UN guards entered Bush's cell, handcuffed and gagged him, and lowered him to the floor. If invading troops were going to extract Bush from the ICC, they would have to do so over their dead bodies.

Immediately upon the Americans' arrival, a firefight broke out with the UN security force entrusted with protecting the ICC.

Loud, rapid, concussive rounds fired by both sides shattered the peace and quiet of the night. Captain Rattigan exchanged close-range fire with one of the soldiers. After a few volleys, Rattigan came to a startling realization. He knew the soldier across from him, Aston Heathcott, an Englishman. They had fought together in the Gulf War. A variety of thoughts flooded Rattigan's mind: The intel he had been given hadn't sufficiently described how formidable a garrison the new ICC Detention Centre was; a successful rescue attempt would require a much bigger force, armed with more weaponry; pursuing this attack any harder might create an international diplomatic disaster for the United States, if it hadn't already; even if they could rescue Bush, he might be wounded or even killed in the crossfire of his own escape; no doubt some of his soldiers would get hit; and, finally, how could he and Heathcott fight each other, having fought so valiantly side by side in Kuwait?

After twenty minutes of nonstop volley exchanges, Captain Rattigan called for a ceasefire, and defying strict military protocol, called out to his friend.

"Aston, is that you, for God's sake?"

Following an awkward pause, Heathcott yelled back, "Yes. Tell me it's not you, Richard."

"I wish I could, my friend," Rattigan replied.

"One hell of an awkward development," Heathcott observed.

"Yep."

"You can't have him, Richard, and the harder you try, the more men you're going to lose."

"Wrong thing to say, Aston, you know that."

"I beg to differ. Just think about it, Richard. A few American soldiers fighting a small army of UN troops? You're not going to get Bush, and the attempt is not worth the lives of your soldiers, or your own life."

As much as Richard Rattigan regretted it, he knew what Aston Heathcott was saying was the plain and simple truth. He and his men were up against a much larger and more heavily equipped opponent, and their chances of rescuing Bush were slim to none.

Breaking the awkward silence, Heathcott questioned, "Richard, I thought the US military's mandate was to protect and defend the United States, not to attack friends on the other side of the world."

While Rattigan considered his friend's remark, Heathcott continued.

"I speak to you now not as a military man, but as a human being to another human being. What is it with America—land of the free, home of the brave—that makes it wage unnecessary and probably illegal wars around the world for no good reason? America is supposed to be a beacon of hope for peace and goodwill to all mankind, not the bully on the block that picks a fight whenever it gets pissed off."

Rattigan had heard enough, and without responding to his friend's taunt, gave the order to his men to retreat, which they did.

Inside the ICC Detention Centre, George W. Bush realized that the prolonged silence after the gunfire meant he wasn't going anywhere, anytime soon. He lay back in his bed, resigned to the fact that he would have to face the consequences of his actions.

Two days later, three members of George W. Bush's defense team waited in the ICC Detention Centre, in a room specifically designed for private prisoner-attorney meetings. The room was windowless and empty except for a rectangular table, six chairs, and two wastebaskets. No guards. No phones. No recording devices. Double-thick walls prevented noise seepage. Seated and reviewing legal briefs were defense attorneys Meredith Lott and Jonathan Ortloff. Lead defense attorney Edward Jamison White III was up and pacing.

Ed White and George Bush had already met and become good buddies in Houston, Texas. Bush had been working in a mentoring program in poverty-stricken communities, and White, a University of Texas graduate with honors, had been cultivating his dreams of becoming a big-time Texas lawyer. As governor of Texas, Bush had assigned White to the prestigious Texas Land Office, where the lawyer would work tirelessly to help fund Texas public schools and provide needed benefits to veterans. Their early fondness for each other had morphed into a lifelong friendship that included wives, kids, deer hunting, baseball games, and the odd business venture.

The door opened. A UN detention guard nodded at former President Bush, who nodded back and entered. White regarded his old friend carefully as he walked over to first shake his hand and then give him a big hug.

"Greetings," Bush said with some relief. "Sorry to have to drag you over here."

"More to the point, I'm sorry they dragged *you* over here. It's the most preposterous thing I ever heard of."

Bush smiled warmly. "Ed, I know how you love your Texas Longhorns during football season. Think they can manage without you?"

White chuckled. "They'll manage, probably better without me there. We have bigger fish to fry." He gestured to his colleagues. "George, I'd like to introduce you to the other two members of your defense team. Both are extraordinary attorneys with impressive credentials. More importantly, they're both schooled and experienced in international criminal law.

"Meredith Lott graduated Phi Beta Kappa from the University of Southern California and first in her class at Stanford Law. She is the top international criminal law attorney at Hurst, Rosenfeld & Felps in Washington, DC, specializing in international extradition, and for good measure she's a black belt in karate. Most folks don't mess with her too much."

Bush offered his hand to shake. "Black belt in karate; my kind of girl."

White continued with his no-nonsense introductions.

"Jonathan Ortloff. Graduated Notre Dame, summa cum laude. His PhD on 'The Creation and Functionality of the International Criminal Court' was published in top law reviews in the United States, Great Britain, and elsewhere in the free world. Jonathan started a boutique law firm in Manhattan that specializes in international law, and is a two handicap at Winged Foot."

Bush shook Ortloff's hand. "Killer attorney with a two handicap at the Foot; where you been all my life?"

"Rest assured, George," White stated confidently, "you've got a million watts of legal capacity here to defend you."

"I don't think this is going to be a fair fight."

"I'm sure the prosecution thinks otherwise. Mind if we jump right in?"

"Can't tell you how much I've been looking forward to doing just that."

After settling into chairs, Ed White looked compassionately at his friend and began.

"First of all, how you doing?"

"I've been better. How the hell can we get me out of here, and how quickly can we do it?"

"'Not sure to the first question, and as soon as legally possible to the second. We need to discuss a number of items, including

ICC protocol and witnesses to call in your defense. But first I want Meredith and Jonathan to share their thoughts relevant to the case in general."

"Okay, bombs away."

"Mr. President," Meredith began, "I'd like to say that my family has loved and supported your family since I was a little girl, and my support for you personally has never wavered."

"Thank you."

"Knowing what you knew at the time, I would've waged war on Iraq as well."

"Gratifying to hear, especially under the circumstances."

"Next, I'd like to state that, in my opinion, the actions taken by the ICC in general, and the prosecutors specifically, are in blatant breach of international legal agreements and violate well-established ethical protocol. Simply put, they are offensive, presumptuous, and arrogant."

Bush nodded. "Agreed," he said.

Next, Jonathan Ortloff spoke.

"President Bush, George, for openers, I'd like to state that the charges alleged against you are not consistent with the generally held understanding of what constitutes war crimes. Furthermore, we have investigated the prosecuting attorneys, McBride and Shadid, and regard them to be inadequate in terms of having the requisite experience or gravitas to effectively prosecute this case, which has potential groundbreaking and precedent-setting legal implications."

Bush raised an eyebrow. "Meaning?"

"Meaning they don't have a chance in hell of making their accusations stick," Meredith chimed in.

"Meaning we're going to kick their butts," Jonathan added.

Bush smiled. "Shit, Ed, these two can play on my team any day."

"Yep, I wouldn't want to try a case against these assassins if I could possibly avoid it," White said confidently and then transitioned to another concern. "George, I'm sure you're worried about Laura."

"More than worried."

"She's okay. Pissed off as hell, but more worried about how you're doing."

"When is she getting here?"

"Soon. Twenty-four hours, tops."

"I'm missing her."

"No doubt." White said, getting down to business. "Now we'd like to lay out our strategy. First, we go on the offense to build your defense."

3

Facing the Music

*"Peace does not mean an absence of conflicts; differences
will always be there. Peace means solving these
differences through peaceful means; through dialogue,
education, knowledge, and through humane ways."*
—Dalai Lama XIV

After a week of educating George W. Bush on international law
and stressing the need to state only the information asked of him
and not volunteer anything more, the defense team notified the
judges they were ready to proceed.

On a crisp September morning in the Netherlands, inside the
International Criminal Court Presiding Judge Harrison Hurst-
Brown rapped his gavel and stated with all due solemnity, "The
trial of George W. Bush is in session. Mr. Bush, have you had
ample time to discuss the case with your defense team such that
you are willing and able to proceed with this trial?"

"Yes and yes," Bush snapped back.

Ed White stood to address the Court. "Your Honors, good
morning. My name is Edward White, and I am Mr. Bush's lead
defense attorney."

Hurst-Brown nodded. "Mr. White, the Court welcomes you."

"Your Honors, with regard to this case, we wish to state here
and now that the ICC has already committed serious breaches of

35

law. Your abduction of a former president of the United States and transference of him against his will here to the ICC is in direct violation of both national and international laws. Accordingly, we hereby request the immediate release of Mr. Bush, after which we will be filing criminal charges against those responsible, including the Office of the Prosecutor, the prosecuting attorneys, and others as warranted."

"Thank you, Mr. White," Hurst-Brown responded, as if he had heard it all before. "We have already addressed the question of jurisdiction in great detail and are satisfied the ICC is within its legal parameters to bring this case against your client. Now, unless you have something new to add, this Court will proceed with what it was created to do."

White amped up the rhetoric. "We're very disappointed to note how entrenched this Court already seems to be, but so be it. Former US President Bush's sovereign immunity stands as a preemptive block against this prosecution. Sovereign immunity has been regarded as a nonnegotiable element in international law since Roman times. Moreover, there is the well-established legal concept known as the War Powers Resolution, which contemplates and embraces a reasonable loss of human life attendant to armed warfare in pursuit of military objectives. You cannot try a duly elected president of the United States for official acts he performed while in office."

Hurst-Brown seemed more than willing to engage in this debate. "Mr. White, the overriding concept here is that Mr. Bush is a former head of state, not a sitting president. You must know that crimes included in the definition of war crimes have no statute of limitations, meaning a suspected perpetrator is libel for such crimes until the day he dies. Now, as there is much to do, Mr. White, I suggest we get on with the business of this Court."

White stood resolute. "Your Honors, we wish to provide warning to this Court that the eyes of the world are watching, and to state emphatically that we consider the Court's actions to be in violation of well-established international law, and in breach of fundamental human rights."

"Your warning is duly noted, Mr. White," Hurst-Brown commented and continued, "it is important for all involved to note that henceforth the defendant in this case, George W. Bush, will be referred to as the accused, and that the term is neutral with regard to guilt or innocence."

"Your Honor," White interrupted again, "the president of the United States is charged with making complicated, challenging, and often controversial decisions. He or she must make these decisions based on what they believe to be in the best interest of their citizens. Here at the ICC, you've dealt with Mr. Bush as if he were a deranged mass murderer—a Slobodan Milošević, Joseph Kony, or even Adolf Hitler—which has resulted in an intensely unfounded and unfair characterization of Mr. Bush that is highly offensive to the American people."

If White had irritated Hurst-Brown, the presiding judge didn't show it. "Thank you for your personal opinion, Mr. White," he said, "but the law is not concerned with whatever else a person may or may not have done during his or her life. Justice is blind. Those of us who are charged with upholding the law seek only the accurate application of the law. Now, with respect, this Court will proceed with the discharge of its solemn duties. Have a seat, Mr. White."

Ed White sat down as Judge Hurst-Brown continued.

"All international cases start with a presumption of innocence. The Rome Statute imposes the burden of proof upon the prosecution, meaning it must prove guilt beyond reasonable doubt. The accused is entitled to a fair, impartial, public, and speedy trial. The accused has the right not to testify against himself, and the silence of the accused cannot be considered in the determination of guilt or innocence. If the accused is found guilty of one or more of the crimes identified within the scope of war crimes, the Court may render punishment in the form of admonishment or imprisonment of up to thirty years, to which may be added a fine. In extreme cases justified by the gravity of the crime or crimes, the Court may impose a term of life imprisonment. However, under no circumstance is this Court authorized to render the death penalty. The decision of this Court will be determined by a majority vote of its three judges: Judge Miyako Kimura of Japan, Judge Omolade Bankole of Nigeria, and I, Harrison Hurst-Brown of the United Kingdom.

"Now, Mr. Bush, the Court would like to provide you with the opportunity to make any comments or ask any questions."

Bush and White exchanged looks, after which White responded. "Mr. Bush has nothing to say at this time."

"Duly noted," Hurst-Brown responded and continued. "Consistent with ICC protocol, the clerk is handing Mr. Bush and defense counsel a document containing the charges that fully define the crimes of which Mr. Bush is accused. Article 7 of the ICC Statute sets forth the definition of crimes against humanity as 'acts committed as part of a widespread or systematic attack against a civilian population including murder, extermination, enslavement, and illegal imprisonment; forcible transfer of population; torture; rape; and persecution of any identifiable group on political, national, ethnic, cultural, religious, or gender grounds.'

"Article 8 states that war crimes include 'willful killing; torture or inhuman treatment; willfully causing great suffering or serious injury to body or health; intentionally launching an attack in the knowledge that such attack will cause incidental loss of life or injury to civilians or damage to civilian objects or widespread, long-term, and severe damage to the natural environment; attacking or bombarding towns, villages, dwellings or buildings which are undefended and not military objectives; willfully depriving prisoners of war the rights of fair and regular trial; prisoner abuse; and intentionally directing attacks against the civilian population not taking direct part in hostilities.'"

Judge Hurst-Brown scanned the courtroom to ensure all had comprehended what he had said, and when confident they had, he continued.

"Now, per Article 64(a), Mr. Bush, we offer you the opportunity to make an admission of guilt."

"I will make no such admission."

"Very well. The Court now recognizes the prosecution in the case of the trial of George W. Bush."

Prosecuting attorney Nadia Shadid nodded to the judges and began.

"Your Honors, Mr. Bush, members of the defense, ICC clerk and staff, greetings. My name is Nadia Shadid. I am from Fallujah in the Iraqi province of Al Anbar, sixty miles outside Baghdad. All of us who care about the International Criminal Court, past, present, and future, are pleased to have this magnificent new building in which to conduct our business. As one might expect, the ICC courtrooms are equipped with state-of-the-art digital equipment. As the ICC has received an unprecedented number of requests from press outlets around the world for coverage of this trial, it is providing, for the first time, live real-time audio and video coverage of the proceedings. Now that we have informed all parties of this coverage, as required by law, we request the Court's permission to commence dissemination of the feed."

"The Court is supportive of providing live coverage of this trial so that interested parties around the world can monitor the case in real time," Hurst-Brown stated proudly, "and approves commencement of the international feed. Thank you, Ms. Shadid."

Shadid looked up to the newly created ICC media room and flashed a thumbs-up. The technicians flipped the switch to engage the new audio and video technology, and then returned the thumbs-up to Shadid as her cue to continue.

"Thank you, Your Honor," she said. "Opening statement from the prosecution will continue from my colleague, Mr. Michael McBride."

McBride nodded at Shadid as she sat and he stood to address the courtroom.

"Your Honors, Mr. Bush, members of the defense team, clerks, guards, courtroom attendants, greetings. To begin, we all must disabuse ourselves of any preconceived notion that just because a man is president of the United States, he is incapable of committing a crime or is immune to international law. That, of course, would have no foundation in logic or law. What follows is a chronological event-by-event story of what George W. Bush did and said in his capacity as president of the United States to cause the Iraq War to happen, bearing in mind that all human lives lost, damage to physical structures, prisoner torture, and maltreatment all are the direct result of his war. Obviously, had Mr. Bush not caused the war to happen, all men and women killed in the war might still be alive, those injured physically and/or mentally would presumably be well, and the damaged or destroyed physical structures would still be standing. And, as there would've been no prisoners, there would have been no prisoner abuse.

"Now, for the orientation of those interested in the facts, I'd like to identify two entirely separate entities. First is the organization known as al Qaeda led by Osama bin Laden; second is the government of Iraq led by its elected president, President Saddam Hussein. As will be clearly proven, Saddam Hussein and Iraq had no working relationship with bin Laden and al Qaeda. They were headquartered in different countries. They were never co-conspirators or co-perpetrators in any activity. In fact, if anything, they were each the enemy of the other.

"Your Honors, the prosecution intends to present facts which provide the foundation of this case, and will prove that George W. Bush is personally responsible for creating the pretext for, and then waging the Iraq War—and the devastating results of his war. From the night of the terrorist attacks on September 11, 2001, to the invasion of Iraq by American troops on March 20, 2003."

Gaining momentum, McBride ramped up his rhetoric. "As history tragically recalls, on September 11, 2001, al Qaeda killed nearly three thousand Americans in attacks at four locations, including the World Trade Center and the Pentagon. Your Honors, the prosecution wishes to submit a chronological record of Mr. Bush's activities from September 11, 2001, to April 20, 2003—the day of the 9/11 attacks to the day of the US invasion of Iraq—which identify more than thirty specific things George W. Bush said or did that shifted attention away from al Qaeda and bin Laden, and directed it toward Iraq and Hussein, eventually leading to the Iraq War."

Judge Hurst-Brown looked at his fellow judges for agreement, and when both nodded in the affirmative, he announced, "Permission granted." Nadia handed a stack of pamphlets to a page, who in turn gave one to the Court recorder and distributed the rest to all pertinent participants.

"On September 11, 2001, the day of the attacks," Michael McBride continued, "the World Trade Center having been reduced to rubble, the Pentagon still burning, a United Airlines plane having crashed into a field near Shanksville, Pennsylvania, President George W. Bush met with his National Coordinator for Security and Infrastructure Protection, Richard A. Clarke, in the White House. Mr. Bush said to Mr. Clarke, 'I know you have a lot to do and all, but I want you, as soon as you can, to go back over everything. See if Saddam did this. See if he's linked in any way.' Clarke responded, 'But, Mr. President, al Qaeda did this.' Bush replied, 'I know, but see if Saddam was involved. Just look. I want to know.' 'Absolutely, we will look,' Clarke answered, 'but you know we have looked several times for state sponsorship of al Qaeda and have not found any real linkage to Iraq.' Then, according to Mr. Clarke, Mr. Bush got testy and said, 'Look into Iraq, Saddam,' and walked away.

"A few days later, after looking into the matter, Mr. Clarke submitted a report signed by all relevant intelligence agencies, including the FBI and the CIA, stating that there was no evidence of Iraqi involvement in 9/11.

"September 21, 2001, ten days after 9/11. Mr. Bush received a classified President's Daily Brief, known as a PDB, indicating that his intelligence team had found no solid evidence linking Saddam Hussein to the September 11 attacks, and that—and I'm quoting from the PDB now—'there was scant credible evidence that Iraq had any significant collaborative ties with al Qaeda.' I repeat for clarification and emphasis, ten days after the attacks on September 11, the defendant received a written report signed by top intelligence officers that stated there was no solid evidence Saddam Hussein or Iraq had any involvement in 9/11, and that there was no credible evidence that Iraq had any ties with al Qaeda.

"November 21, 2001, two months and ten days after the 9/11 attacks, during a National Security Council meeting in the White

House, Mr. Bush asked Secretary of Defense Donald Rumsfeld to review existing battle plans for Iraq. Quoting Bush: 'What kind of war plan do you have for Iraq?' Rumsfeld said he would look into it. Then the defendant said, 'And get Tommy Franks looking at what it would take to protect America by removing Saddam Hussein if we have to.' Please note that it was on this day, November 21, 2001, one year and four months before the invasion of Iraq, that George W. Bush first put into motion the series of events that would lead to his war.

"On August 5, 2002, Mr. Bush met with Secretary of State Colin Powell and National Security Advisor Condoleezza Rice in the White House. Secretary Powell, a decorated Army general with a public approval rating of 70 percent, was troubled, stating, 'War could destabilize friendly regimes in the region: Saudi Arabia, Egypt, and Jordan. War would take down Saddam and you will become the governing force until you get a new government. You break it, you own it. It's nice to say we can do it unilaterally, except we can't. Worse, the United States, in perhaps the largest manhunt in history, has not found Osama bin Laden.'"

McBride turned to address the judges directly. "Please, Your Honors, there should be no doubt that George W. Bush used the attacks of 9/11 as a justification for his war with Iraq, even though the one had absolutely nothing to do with the other."

White interrupted. "Objection, Your Honors. Conjecture."

Hurst-Brown agreed. "Objection sustained. Mr. McBride, stick to the facts and withhold your personal interpretation of the events."

Michael McBride responded the only way he could. "Yes, sir. Sorry, sir."

Sensing an opportunity to break the prosecution's momentum, White interrupted. "Your Honors, given the lateness of the hour, defense requests a suspension to the day's proceedings."

Hurst-Brown glanced at the other judges, who nodded their approval, and announced, "Court is adjourned until 9:00 AM tomorrow."

As soon as this historic day of the Bush trial had ended, the BBC cut to its news studio on Portland Place in London, where Elizabeth Reynolds and Sir Nigel Pemberton sat in front of six cameras. After Reynolds welcomed her audience, she quickly turned to her friend and legal expert.

"Sir Nigel, what do we make of day one of the trial of Geroge W. Bush?"

"In my opinion, the most important things are those that did not get mentioned, Elizabeth, more than those that did."

"Sir Nigel, I will be very pleased to have you explain that," Reynolds said, raising an eyebrow.

"According to international law as set forth in Article 17 of the Rome Statute, there is a concept known as the complimentary rule, which provides that the ICC shall determine that a case is inadmissible, and I am now quoting, 'where the case is being investigated or prosecuted by a State which has jurisdiction over it, unless the State is unwilling or unable genuinely to carry out the investigation or prosecution.'"

"In other words," Reynolds clarified, "the State, which in this case refers to the United States, has first rights to a trial if it wants it, not the ICC."

"Correct," Sir Nigel answered, "but Article 17 also states that if 'there has been an unjustified delay in the proceedings which is inconsistent with an intent to bring the person concerned to justice,' then the jurisdiction may revert to the International Criminal Court."

Reynolds, intending to make sure her audience was following, inserted two facts. "The Iraq War ended in December of 2011, and George W. Bush has not yet been brought to trial in America."

Sir Nigel nodded. "The legal justification the ICC Prosecutors engaged was that, as the USA had not brought George W. Bush to trial for suspected crimes committed during the Iraq War, and sufficient time had passed, these two facts allowed the ICC to assume legal jurisdiction of the case, commence investigation, and ultimately start this trial."

"Fascinating, Sir Nigel, but Americans are not stupid," Reynolds said. "One wonders why they haven't simply invoked the complementarity rule and brought George W. Bush back home."

"Ay, there's the rub. For if the United States were to do that, it would also be recognizing the jurisdictional authority of the ICC, and essentially international law over national law, something it has steadfastly refused to do, and frankly something I cannot see it doing even now."

Reynolds paused a moment and said, "So we can conclude that all people, whether American or otherwise, should be more knowledgeable and supportive of international law, as it may be the only system of rules available to prevent headstrong leaders around the world from dragging their countries into war."

On an evening news program in Russia that night, one of its most respected political pundits, Anatoly Vetrov of NTV, offered his take, stating, "The obvious explanation of why the United States is not a member of the International Criminal Court, even though its closest allies, the United Kingdom, France, Australia, and Canada are, must be that George Bush Jr. suspected he would commit crimes that would violate international law and didn't want to face trial and punishment at the ICC. The Bush case is significant because it would set a precedent that all leaders of all countries, whether members of the ICC or not, could be held to the rigid standards of international criminal law."

This commentary from a Russian journalist was of particular interest, as the list of non-signatory countries to the ICC included China, North Korea, Iran, Syria, and Russia.

Following a night of heated discussion and debate among the teams of attorneys regarding the early going of the case, the Court reassembled at its designated hour. Intent on regaining the momentum he had created the previous day, prosecuting attorney Michael McBride began.

"Continuing with the litany of specific statements and actions done by the defendant George W. Bush to cause the Iraq War," McBride said, "I call your attention, Your Honors, to a report entitled 'Iraq: Status of WMD Programs,' written by the head of the Joint Staff's intelligence team, Air Force Major General Glen Shaffer, six and a half months before the defendant sent America into war with Iraq. In it, Major General Shaffer states that—and I'm quoting now—'we don't know with any precision how much we don't know'; 'our knowledge of the Iraqi weapons program is based largely, perhaps 90 percent, on analysis of imprecise intelligence'; 'our assessments rely heavily on analytic assumptions and judgment rather than hard evidence'; 'we do not know with confidence the location of any nuclear weapon-related facilities'; and finally, 'we cannot confirm the identity of any Iraqi facilities that produce, test, fill, or store biological weapons.'

"Now, Mr. Bush," McBride said, turning to the former president, "I believe there's an old saying in Texas: 'If it looks like a skunk and smells like a skunk, then it's a skunk.' This report was commissioned by Secretary of Defense Donald Rumsfeld and compiled by the Joint Staff's intelligence team. Information such as this makes it easy to understand why you may refuse to testify in this Court under oath, because when questioned, either you would have to admit you weren't aware of it, thus exposing gross dereliction of duty, or confess you were aware of it, which would prove you waged the Iraq War in the knowledge that you did not have legal justification. While you are within your rights not to testify, Mr. Bush, your silence may and hopefully will be perceived as an admission of guilt."

"Objection, Your Honors," White barked. "You've already instructed that, under international law, refusal to testify is not to be considered an admission of guilt."

Hurst-Brown could only concur. "Objection sustained."

"Those who have nothing to hide and are convinced the truth is on their side are only too happy to testify in their defense," McBride said.

"Mr. McBride, I caution you to leave your personal opinions outside this court of law," Hurst-Brown chided.

McBride noted the admonition and continued.

"On September 19, 2002, Mr. Bush met with eleven members of the House of Representatives and stated, 'The biggest threat is Saddam Hussein and his weapons of mass destruction.' Fact: The last time there was proof Saddam had WMD was in the mid-1990s, more than ten years earlier. He certainly did not have WMD in 2002, as Mr. Bush threatened he did, as was clearly and abundantly proven later by many reliable sources.

"Of Saddam Hussein, the defendant also said, 'He can blow up Israel and that would trigger an international conflict.' Blow up Israel! Really? Under the circumstances that existed at that time, it would have been virtually impossible for Saddam to transport bomb tonnage sufficient to blow up Israel, even if he had possessed it. Saddam had virtually no friends in the region to help with such an attack, having fought with most of them for years, and besides, many of them were friendly to the United States, a steadfast friend of Israel. Mr. Bush also said, 'We will take over the oil fields and mitigate the shock.' This was another piece of Bush's strategy: Use America's fear of an oil shortage in the Middle East and rising gas prices at home to convince the American people of the need for his war.

"On September 26, 2002, five months and twenty-four days before the war, Mr. Bush met with eighteen congressmen in the White House, stating, 'Saddam Hussein is a terrible guy who is teaming up with al Qaeda.' Not so. We've already provided evidence that numerous government agencies informed Mr. Bush in writing that neither Saddam nor Iraq had any connection to, or affiliation with, al Qaeda. What George W. Bush was telling US congressmen was not true. As there was never evidence connecting Saddam to al Qaeda, there was never legal or legitimate justification to wage his war."

It was hard to tell whether defense attorney White's objections were genuine, in the sense that he felt McBride was out of bounds, or cosmetic, in the sense that he wanted to stop McBride's momentum. Nonetheless, White continued the practice.

"Objection, Your Honors. It is totally preposterous that the prosecution could state such things so unequivocally without having firsthand access to secret classified government documents that would be available to a sitting president."

Hurst-Brown turned toward the prosecutor. "Mr. McBride?"

McBride responded instantly. "Following the Iraq War, the United States government conducted two comprehensive investigations of what was known, when it was known, and by whom it was known. All information on the matter, whether classified or otherwise, is now publically available, and all principal players in and attendant to the White House at the time have published memoirs detailing what happened before, during, and after the war. The facts are available to anybody who bothers to look, regardless of the defense's attempt to make them seem obscure or classified. In light of this easily accessible information, it is not unreasonable to say that Mr. Bush fabricated, or grossly exaggerated known facts while beating the drum for his war. Nonetheless, a lie by any other name is still a lie."

"Objection overruled," Hurst-Brown answered. "Mr. McBride, you may continue."

"Thank you, Your Honor. Mr. Bush further incriminated himself when he commented to another group of congressmen on September 26, 2002, saying, 'It is clear Saddam has weapons of mass destruction—anthrax, VX—and still needs plutonium, and he has not been shy about trying to find it. Time frame for Iraq having a nuke would be six months.'

"Following his White House meetings with selected members of Congress, the defendant engaged in another critical part of his strategy: Fearmongering to the American people. In a primetime speech from Cincinnati, Ohio, on October 7, 2002, five months and thirteen days before the war, he said, 'Iraq gathers the most serious dangers of our age in one place. The danger is already significant, and it only grows worse with time. Facing clear evidence of peril, we cannot wait for the final proof, the "smoking gun" that could come in the form of a mushroom cloud.' These statements and many others prove conclusively that Mr. Bush engaged in an orchestrated propaganda campaign to brainwash and frighten the American people into believing there was a clear and present danger that the United States would be attacked by Iraq. Yet again, there was no truth to what Mr. Bush was telling the American people and the world, as was proven during and after the war.

"On October 10, 2002, five months and ten days before the war, based on Mr. Bush's campaign of misinformation and lies, the US House of Representatives passed a resolution authorizing him to use armed forces in Iraq, but only to 'defend national security.' The resolution stated, 'The president is authorized to use the Armed Forces of the United States as he determines to be necessary and appropriate in order to defend the national security of the United States against the continuing threat posed by Iraq.' Note the resolution said, 'defend the national security of the United States.' Let me state the truth clearly for the record. *Iraq never attacked, or threatened to attack, or even had the capacity to attack the United States.* The threat of Iraq attacking America was never a reality, but fear of such an attack was cleverly drummed up by the defendant.

"In early November 2002, four and a half months before the war, Mr. Bush met in the White House with Hans Blix, head of the UN Iraq weapons inspection team. Bush said, 'You've got to understand, Mr. Blix, you've got the force of the United States behind you. And I'm prepared to use it if need be to enforce this resolution. The decision to go to war will be my decision.'"

McBride turned to the judges to emphasize his point. "Your Honors, please note, Mr. Bush said, 'The decision to go to war will be my decision.' He was correct in saying that. As president and commander in chief, it was his decision, and he must face the consequences of such a decision.

"In late November 2002, three months and three weeks before the war, UN weapons inspectors began inspections in Iraq, unopposed by Saddam or any other Iraqis. Seven hundred and thirty-one UN inspections took place and yielded nothing. I repeat,

UN inspections in Iraq taking place over nearly four months and allowed by Saddam found no WMD or any other offending weaponry.

"On January 27, 2003, one month and twenty-two days before the Iraq war, a United Nations Security Council report by the director general of the International Atomic Energy Agency, Mohamed ElBaradei, stated, 'We have found no evidence that Iraq has revived its nuclear weapons program since its elimination of the program in the 1990s. We should be able within the next few months to provide credible assurance that Iraq has no nuclear program.'"

McBride turned yet again to the judges. "Your Honors, please take note of this: Fifty-two days before the invasion, the International Atomic Energy Agency said it had found no evidence that Saddam had nuclear weapons. But anxious for his war, Mr. Bush got desperate.

"On February 7, 2003, one month and thirteen days before the war, French President Jacques Chirac called Mr. Bush to offer guidance. 'I don't share your spirit for why we need war. War is not inevitable. There are alternative ways to reach our goals,' he said. Mr. Bush responded by saying, 'I view an armed Saddam Hussein as a direct threat to the American people.'

"On February 10, 2003, forty days before the war, French President Chirac, German Chancellor Gerhard Schröder, and Russian President Vladimir Putin issued a joint statement, which called for extended United Nations weapons inspections in Iraq. Chirac stated emphatically, 'Nothing today justifies war. Russia, Germany, and France are determined to ensure that everything possible is done to disarm Iraq peacefully.'

"On February 14, 2003, thirty-six days before the war, Hans Blix presented his findings to the UN Security Council, stating, 'Since we arrived in Iraq, we have conducted more than four hundred inspections covering more than three hundred sites. More than two hundred chemical and one hundred biological samples have been collected and no prohibited weapons or substances have been found.' Please note that the defendant learned about this, and thus knew about this, thirty-six days before he ordered the invasion of Iraq, plenty of time for him to have stopped his war, or at least to have postponed it.

"On March 5, 2003, fifteen days before the war, Mr. Bush met with an envoy sent by Pope John Paul II, Cardinal Pio Laghi, whose message was, 'There would be civilian casualties and it would deepen the gulf between the Christian world and the Muslim world. It would not be a just war. It would be illegal and it would not make things better.' George W. Bush responded, 'Absolutely it will make things better.'

"On March 16, 2003, four days before the war, French President Chirac was interviewed on the highly regarded CBS news program *60 Minutes,* during which he called for UN inspectors in Iraq to be given another thirty days. Bush then commented on Chirac's request for patience by saying, 'It's a delaying tactic,' and gave Saddam and his two sons forty-eight hours to get out of Iraq, adding, 'the Iraqi regime will disarm itself, or the Iraqi regime will be resolved by force.'

"On March 19, 2003, the day before the war, at 5:00 AM EST, in Washington, DC, George W. Bush addressed his National Security Council in the White House, saying, 'Do you have any last comments, recommendations, or thoughts?' No one did. Nevertheless, Mr. Bush pronounced, 'For the sake of peace in the world, and security for our country and the rest of the free world, and for the freedom of the Iraqi people, I give Secretary Rumsfeld the order to execute Operation Iraqi Freedom,' thus providing clear and irrefutable evidence once and for all that George W. Bush personally ordered the war in Iraq, and must personally accept the responsibility for the death and damage caused by his war."

McBride turned to address the defendant. "Mr. Bush, there were no winners in your war, only losers."

"No winners?" Bush fired back as he leapt to his feet. He had listened to McBride's litany with little interest, but this last comment was more than he could bear. "Saddam Hussein is a dead man now, and Iraq has got about thirty-four million people who no longer live under his tyranny."

"Order in the Court," Hurst-Brown said, rapping his gavel.

Ed White grabbed Bush's arm to restrain him, but the defendant wasn't finished with McBride.

"You can't just recite a bunch of out-of-context, unfounded bullshit and expect anybody to take you seriously," Bush said.

Hurst-Brown had had enough. "Mr. White, either your client shows some respect for this Court or we will find him in contempt. Do I make myself clear?"

"Apologies, Your Honors," Ed White responded. "These were difficult times, and people have strong opinions and even stronger emotions. Respectfully, we apologize to the Court."

"Apology accepted, Mr. White," Hurst-Brown replied, "but ensure it doesn't happen again. Prosecution, you may continue."

McBride restarted his assault.

"On March 20, 2003, one year, six months, and nine days after the 9/11 attacks, and after George W. Bush had started his drumbeat for war, he got his war. US-led Special Operations Forces invaded Iraq."

Intending to let his litany of accusations linger in the room, Michael McBride paused for nearly thirty seconds before continuing.

"Your Honors, I would like to clearly define and emphasize the magnitude of the defendant's distortion of the truth. Following his war, the Center for Public Integrity stated, 'It is beyond dispute that Iraq did not possess any weapons of mass destruction, or have meaningful ties to al Qaeda.' The report listed nine hundred and thirty-five false statements made by Mr. Bush and his closest aides regarding the security risk posed by Iraq during the time following the attacks of 9/11 and the Iraq War in March 2003. The report confirms that the defendant personally made two hundred and thirty-two false statements about Iraq and Saddam Hussein, and twenty-eight false statements about Iraq's links to al Qaeda. As a direct result of the defendant's campaign of lies, fearmongering and warmongering, an assault force of 250,000 US and coalition forces invaded the sovereign country of Iraq."

McBride turned to the judges. "Your Honors, on this very day of shame, George W. Bush addressed the American people live on primetime television, saying, 'American and coalition forces are in early stages of military operations to disarm Iraq.' Of what? No one found WMD because there weren't any. Mr. Bush maintained he was doing this 'to free its people' without having the slightest idea of what to do with the Iraqi people once he removed Saddam—a lack of judgment that created a monumental problem that plagues the world even to this day. The defendant, George W. Bush, for whatever distorted, convoluted, misinformed reasons, had it all wrong."

Hoping to preempt an objection from the defense, McBride turned quickly to Bush. "Your war created an enormous amount of anger around the world, leading to huge protests in six hundred cities. The protestors counted among their number three million people in Rome, one million in London, and hundreds of thousands in New York City and Paris. This worldwide protest against your war was the largest global protest event in human history."

With increasing theatricality, McBride turned back to the judges. "Your Honors, a fundamental principle of international law is that countries are prohibited from using military force except in self-defense. Quite obviously the United States did not act in self-defense, because Iraq didn't invade, or have the intention or capacity to invade. And not only did the United States not have authorization from the Security Council, but by a vote of eleven to four it specifically opposed military action.

"And so we can see and understand the facts, and thus know the truth. The evidence is chronological, plentiful, clear, and conclusive that this man sitting before you, George W. Bush, is the single person most responsible for causing the Iraq War. It all started with him. It couldn't have happened without him. And now he must accept the responsibility for the death and destruction resulting from his war. Following the 9/11 attacks, Mr. Bush used his nation's emotional wounds and desire for revenge to attack Iraq and topple Saddam Hussein—instead of taking out Osama bin Laden and al Qaeda, which is what he should have done. Other than Hitler's horrific crimes in connection with World War II, the ICC may never have such a clear, open-and-shut case against a single perpetrator of such horrific, destructive, unnecessary, and illegal war crimes as this man, George W. Bush.

"Your Honors, I pray for the peoples of Iraq, indeed for all the peoples of the world, that you see the Iraq War for what it was, and this man for what he did. If leaders of superpowers are allowed to wage unnecessary and illegal wars with impunity, humankind is doomed to experience more such disastrous wars in the future. That said, George Bush couldn't and didn't do it alone. Your

Honors, as is well known, the ICC first seeks to bring to justice the one person most responsible for causing the crime or crimes to occur. It also provides that each co-conspirator must stand trial for his or her role in the commission of these crimes. We want to make abundantly clear that George Bush's co-conspirators in the creation and waging of the Iraq War, including Vice President Dick Cheney, National Security Advisor Condoleezza Rice, Secretary of Defense Donald Rumsfeld, and Deputy Secretary of Defense Paul Wolfowitz, will be the focus of further investigations and, if warranted, prosecution."

McBride paused to let his comments linger in the Court once again. No one spoke. No one moved. Finally, he concluded simply by saying, "Your Honors, the prosecution rests."

"Thank you, Mr. McBride," Judge Kimura responded. "At this time the Court will take a thirty-minute break after which we invite defense counsel to offer its opening statement on behalf of the defendant."

No clear thinking person in or outside the United States thought that America would stand idly by as a former president was being tried at the ICC. The United States had insisted on an emergency meeting of the permanent members of the UN Security Council—China, France, Russia, the United Kingdom, and the United States. Following much heated debate, the majority vote had come down against having the UN override the jurisdiction of the ICC relative to the administration of international law, which meant the Bush trial would continue.

The United States had to come to terms with the fact that whatever it did, it would do so unilaterally and without the support of its traditional allies. Following the failed attempt by Special

Operations Forces to rescue Mr. Bush, the US military brass had pivoted to Plan B: Move one of its supercarriers, coincidentally the USS *George H. W. Bush,* into the hostile theater. The battleship, named after the 41st president, had been built in 2009 at a cost of 6.2 billion dollars, and was well equipped with ninety fixed-wing aircraft and an assortment of helicopters.

The USS *George H. W. Bush* had been patrolling the coasts off Turkey and Syria in the eastern waters of the Mediterranean when the order was given. Traveling at speeds in excess of thirty knots, she made her way west across the Mediterranean, turned north at the Atlantic Ocean, moved through the English Channel, and arrived at her destination in the North Sea, within clear eyesight of The Hague and two miles from the International Criminal Court.

Of course, the unannounced arrival of a US battleship off the coast of The Hague had caught the attention of virtually everybody, precisely its intention. Since the Americans hadn't asked permission, and weren't announcing their intentions, all opinions were merely speculation. Some journalists theorized that the US military would not tolerate a guilty verdict from the ICC, and would launch a massive rescue attempt in response. Others held that George W. Bush had waged the Iraq War, and battleship or no battleship, if he was found to be a criminal under international law, then he must comply with his sentence.

Proceeding with its business, the Court reassembled following its brief break. After being called by Judge Kimura, defense attorney Ed White nodded confidently at Bush and stood to make his opening statement.

"Thank you, Your Honor. First, and let me be clear about this, what the International Criminal Court has done, and is doing, to a former president of the United States is placing its very existence in jeopardy. Article 55(2) of the Rome Statute requires a person being arrested to be informed of the basis of their arrest, their right to remain silent without such silence being considered as guilt or innocence, and the right to counsel, essentially the equivalent of America's Miranda warning. Your commandos scooped up Mr. Bush off a golf course in Scotland and deposited him into your custody. Anyone who knows international law is aware that the bounty hunter technique used to abduct the defendant, along with failing to inform him properly of his rights, is not only reprehensible in and of itself, but serves to prejudice the case."

In a not too subtle attempt to ensure his many points had been understood by those who mattered most, and to set the stage for his big finish, Ed White took a long sip of water before continuing.

"Furthermore, as a legal precedent, it should be noted that American presidents in the twentieth century alone have waged wars in Korea, Vietnam, and Kuwait, and have done so with impunity. The US Constitution makes it the job of the president to protect the Republic, and Mr. Bush, like all presidents before him, was doing his constitutionally mandated job. Moreover, international law is based entirely on consent, and the United States has not signed any document that recognizes the ICC's jurisdiction over its citizens. Thus, based on a lack of judicial authority, the illegal kidnapping of the defendant, and a failure to notify him of his rights, defense moves for dismissal of this case and the immediate release of former President George W. Bush, at which time he will be escorted back to America, where he belongs."

Nadia Shadid leapt to her feet. "Objection, Your Honors. Blatant disregard and disrespect for this Court and for international justice."

"Objection noted," Judge Hurst-Brown responded. "Ms. Shadid, please be seated."

She hesitated a beat too long.

"Your objection is noted, Ms. Shadid, now sit down," Hurst-Brown repeated.

She sat.

Hurst-Brown turned his attention back to the lead defense attorney. "Now, Mr. White, about your request. Up until now, the ICC has relied upon member states and their traditional police forces to effectuate its arrest warrants. The military operation used in this case departs from that practice, and you are correct to raise the point. However, most courts, and indeed American courts after the Supreme Court decision in Alvarez-Machain, do not question how suspected criminals come before them when arriving from abroad. Consequently, your motion is denied. Any further comments or questions?"

"Yes, we have a lot more to ask and say, Your Honor," White responded, "but respectfully, the defense requests a continuance until tomorrow afternoon."

"Very well, Mr. White. Request granted," Hurst-Brown pronounced after getting visual approval from his fellow judges and rapping his gavel. "The Prosecutor v. George W. Bush is adjourned until 2:00 PM tomorrow afternoon."

4

Eye of the Storm

*"What good fortune for governments
that the people do not think."*

—ADOLF HITLER

THE HAGUE IN THE NETHERLANDS WAS DEEMED to be the city of international justice in 1899 when it hosted the world's first peace conference. In the early twentieth century, the Scottish-American millionaire steel magnate Andrew Carnegie built the Peace Palace in The Hague to house the Permanent Court of Arbitration. The PCA, as it's referred to, is not a court per se, but rather provides services to resolve international disputes arising between feuding organizations or private parties. And so it was no surprise that, when the United Nations sought a city to be the permanent home of the International Criminal Court, The Hague was its de facto choice.

It was here in The Hague that Mrs. George W. Bush, the former first lady of the United States, arrived after a long but uneventful journey. Starting in Crawford, Texas, a convoy of Secret Service officers loaded Mrs. Bush and her luggage into a black SUV and transported her to a nearby airport, where she boarded a US government Gulfstream for a flight to Washington, DC. At Dulles Airport she was hustled onto a KLM flight bound nonstop for Amsterdam. For privacy and security reasons, the State Department had taken over the entire first-class cabin, having displaced other passengers to either business class or later flights. Mrs. Bush settled into seat

1A with two Secret Service officers and two Special Ops Marines seated in the rows behind her. After a pleasant but mostly uneaten dinner, she closed her eyes for what would understandably be a fitful night's sleep.

Laura Bush was born Laura Lane Welch on November 4, 1946, in the boom-or-bust town of Midland, Texas. Her father served his country valiantly as a member of the 105th Army Battalion, which liberated the German town of Nordhausen, site of a Nazi concentration camp that housed five thousand prisoners. Laura graduated from Southern Methodist University in Dallas, and then from the University of Texas in Austin, where she earned her master's degree in library science. She returned home to Midland to work as a school librarian until she met and married George W. Bush in 1977. Although he was raised Episcopalian, George converted to Laura's Methodist faith and they were married in the First Methodist Church.

When Laura arrived in The Hague, she checked into Hotel Des Indes, an old world hostelry considered one of the best in the city, dropped off her luggage, and was whisked off to the ICC Detention Centre along with a suitcase full of her husband's clothes and accessories.

Mr. Bush was pacing around a table in the middle of a meeting room when the door opened and Laura entered. A long welcoming hug was followed by many questions: How are you doing? What happened? Can the ICC do this? Next they talked about their twin daughters, Barbara and Jenna (named after their grandmothers, Barbara Bush and Jenna Welch). At last, Laura asked the all-important question.

"How's the trial going?"

"It's going, that's the first problem," George answered.

"Meaning?"

"Meaning I never should've been brought here in the first place."

"Can't Ed White get you out of this mess?"

"He tried."

"And?"

"I'm still here."

"George," Laura said, shaking her head, "there has to be something we can do."

"Honestly, we *are* doing everything we can. I got a great team of lawyers and justice is on our side. There's no way any rational court in the world could find me guilty of war crimes."

"Including the ICC?"

"Including the ICC."

Laura studied her husband's eyes. "I pray to God you're right."

Their conversation eventually turned to an incident that occurred in April 2001, when British Prime Minister Tony Blair and his wife, Cherie, were visiting the Bushes at their ranch in Crawford. Mrs. Blair used the occasion to plea with Mr. Bush to reconsider his opposition to the International Criminal Court, and to take the necessary steps to have the United States rejoin. After all, she argued, the United Kingdom, France, Canada, and other powerful allies of the United States were members; why not the United States? Nonetheless, Mr. Bush dismissed Mrs. Blair's request.

Having not forgotten that conversation, Laura wondered aloud.

"George, would we be sitting here today if you didn't have the United States resign its membership of the ICC?"

Mr. Bush considered the question for a moment.

"No, it may have happened even sooner," he said. "Let's not forget, the UK is a member of the ICC and the Brits leveled charges against Tony Blair in English courts."

After an hour, per ICC prison protocol, the meeting of George and Laura Bush came to an end. Laura lifted a Bible from her purse, and opened it to a preselected passage.

"Here, darling. We should read this," she said.

George took the book, shared a loving moment with his wife, and read aloud.

"Proverbs 3:33. The curse of the Lord is on the house of the wicked, but he blesses the home of the just. Surely he scorns the scornful, but gives grace to the humble. The wise shall inherit glory, but shame shall be the legacy of fools," he said solemnly.

The Hague features pleasant walks, interesting but smallish boutiques and hotels, and a collection of inviting watering holes that provides food and drink for the many internationals that work at the ICC. One of the most popular is Paraplu, Dutch for "umbrella." Michael McBride and Nadia Shadid sat in the back corner of the restaurant, picking at bites of roasted lamb and sipping a French burgundy. Nadia broke a lingering silence by saying softly, "The tragedy of this, of course, is that we shouldn't be having this trial."

Michael cocked his head, indicating he wasn't quite sure what she was talking about.

"There shouldn't have been a war in the first place," she continued. "Iraq is another Vietnam. What is it about America, or at least some Americans, that makes them want to enforce democracy on other countries that do not want it? Vietnam, Iraq, what's next?"

Michael took a swig of wine, considering the question. "I don't have a suitable answer for your question," he said, "but all sane Americans should do everything in their power to oppose the war machine and ensure there are no more Vietnams or Iraqs."

"A second tragedy is that my country was punished way out of proportion to what Saddam may or may not have been doing at the time," Nadia pressed on.

"He sure had done plenty of horrible things in the past, yes, but what was he actually doing at the time to deserve that war?" Michael asked.

"Ironically, he was writing his fourth book. The English translation would be *Get Out of Here, Curse You!* He finished it two days before the US invasion."

Michael's puzzled look revealed he had not been aware of that.

"It's incredible that a country with the rich heritage of Iraq could fall into such modern-day despair," Nadia said.

Michael felt a profound sadness for Nadia, and for all Iraqi people. "My sincere hope is that one day your country will return to its former glory," he said.

"A noble wish devoutly to be desired, however unlikely it might be," Nadia said.

Late summer in the Netherlands had turned to autumn, although it felt more like early winter, with some pedestrians even wearing scarves and hats. Nonstop gavel-to-gavel live audio and video streaming of The Prosecutor v. George W. Bush had been well received by massive audiences around the world, so much so that in a next-generation attempt to be more transparent, the ICC came up with something entirely new in the world of jurisprudence. As public viewing galleries at the ICC seated only about two hundred and twenty people, the Court commissioned the installation of three huge video monitors outside the building for public viewing. The monitors were placed at strategic locations, each turned in a different direction, to service those who could not gain access to the public gallery inside. Both public and press likened the new

ICC monitors to those outside Centre Court at Wimbledon, and at popular music concerts. International criminal law had become high-tech and mainstream.

At the designated hour, the Court re-adjourned for day three of the Bush trial. Outside, thousands were gathering to watch the trial for the first time on the new large-screen monitors. Inside, the public gallery was packed to the gills, as usual. But on this occasion, the audience included an American woman much camouflaged but unmistakably Mrs. George W. Bush. In the crowded courtroom below, the clerk announced, "All rise." All did except George Bush and his defense team. Three ICC judges—Harrison Hurst-Brown of England, Miyako Kimura of Japan, and Omolade Bankole of Nigeria—entered and sat, as did all others in the courtroom.

Presiding Judge Hurst-Brown began the day's proceeding.

"The International Criminal Court is now in session. The Prosecutor v. George W. Bush. Defense counsel may continue with its opening statement."

Lead defense attorney Edward White, dressed fashionably in a gray suit with contrasting pink tie, restarted his defense.

"Thank you, Your Honor. Good day, everybody. Ironclad evidence in the intelligence business is scarce and, as such, experienced weapons analysts are often forced to make 'informed judgments.' During the period before the Iraq War, evidence regarding Iraq's military capacity was confusing and contradictory, precisely because Saddam Hussein had made it so.

"It is factually true that no one found definitive proof that Iraq had biological weapons or weapons of mass destruction. Yet, coupled with the incontrovertible proof that Saddam had such weapons in the past, a conclusion that he still had them seemed obvious, especially as he was a notorious liar, manipulator, criminal, and cheat. The opposing view was that Saddam didn't have such weapons. But to arrive at that conclusion, much accumulated intelligence would have to have been ignored. The most sensible conclusion was that he probably had WMD, and who in their right minds would dare to bet he didn't?

"Putting the evidence or lack of evidence aside, there were many reasons why George Bush had justification for the Iraq War. First, to resolve certain unanswered questions left after the first Bush administration, when in 1991 after the Gulf War, it let Saddam Hussein consolidate power and slaughter opponents. Second, to protect America's closest allies in the region including Israel, and to improve its strategic position by eliminating a hostile enemy. Third, to permit the withdrawal of US forces from Saudi Arabia, where they had been stationed for decades. Fourth, to quiet anti-American rhetoric that threatened America's allies in the region. Fifth, to create another source of oil for the US market, namely Iraq, and thus reduce dependency on oil from Saudi Arabia. Sixth, to help transition an important Middle Eastern country ruled by a ruthless dictator into a pro-American democracy capable in time of functioning under free elections and the rule of law. Seventh, to create a democracy in the region that could serve as a model to other friendly Arab states, notably Egypt and Saudi Arabia. And finally, and perhaps most importantly, to protect and defend the American people both at home and abroad in a new era of global terrorism.

"So, upon fair and dispassionate analysis, George W. Bush would not have been fulfilling his obligations to protect and defend the United States of America if he had not gone to war with Iraq."

Gaining momentum, White turned to address the ICC judges.

"However much the ICC considers its legal imperative to protect the citizens of the world, I assure it that the president of the

United States considers his constitutional imperative to protect his own citizens of equal importance. Under international humanitarian law, and the Rome Statute itself, for that matter, the death of civilians during an armed conflict, no matter how grave and regrettable, does not in and of itself constitute a war crime. International law permits an opposing country to carry out proportional attacks against military objectives, even when it is known that some civilian deaths or injuries will occur. A crime occurs only if there is an intentional attack directed against a civilian population, and such was definitely not the case in the Iraq War.

"Moreover, there are many fundamental principles of international criminal law that, when considered individually and collectively, expressly preclude the trying of this case against former President Bush. While all crimes within the jurisdiction of the Court would seem to be grave, the Rome Statute requires an additional threshold of gravity for war crimes, as set forth in Article 8(1), which states that 'the Court shall have jurisdiction in respect of war crimes in particular when committed as part of a plan or policy or as part of a large-scale commission of such crimes.'

"Informed people familiar with this case know the Iraq War was not, and was never intended to be, a large-scale invasion of the country. Defense will prove that this criterion for war crimes is not satisfied in this case. However, even if one were to assume that Article 8(1) had been satisfied, it would then be necessary to consider the messy issues of jurisdiction, admissibility, the rule of complementarity, and other legal matters attendant to this case. Furthermore, Article 8(2) criminalizes an attack by an opposing nation only in the knowledge that such an attack will cause incidental loss of life or injury to civilians, damage to civilian objects, or widespread and severe damage to the natural environment that would be clearly excessive in relation to the direct overall military advantage anticipated. Available evidence does establish that civilians died or were injured during the subject military operations. But such information does not indicate coalition forces specifically attacked the civilian population, or that they were clearly excessive in relation to the military advantage gained.

"All available evidence is to be measured by the existence of information that monitored excessiveness in relation to military advantage gained. Publicly available information from the United States and the United Kingdom provides evidence of compliance to the above, as follows: First, a list of potential targets was identified in advance. Second, commanders had legal advice available to them at all times and were made aware of the need to comply with international humanitarian law, including the principles of proportionality. Third, detailed computer modeling was used in assessing targets. Fourth, political, legal and military oversight was established for target approval. This information has not been contradicted by any source and thus perforce must be taken into consideration in accordance with customary legal evaluation. The defense will prove conclusively that approximately 85 percent of the weapons used by coalition aircraft were precision guided, which confirms the effort to minimize casualties. Thus, the available information does not allow for the conclusion that a clearly excessive crime within the jurisdiction of the Court has been committed.

"And finally, the United States and the United Kingdom were joined by thirty-eight other countries from around the world, which all participated in the Iraq war effort. Would it be the intention of the ICC to hold accountable all the leaders of all those countries? If the leaders of forty countries believed that the Iraq War was justifiable, how can the International Criminal Court determine it was not? Thank you, Your Honors. The defense rests."

Ed White nodded at George Bush as he sat.

The prosecution couldn't risk inaction after the defense had gained such critical ground. After exchanging nods with McBride, Nadia Shadid addressed the judges.

"Your Honors, the prosecution requests permission to respond."

"Permission granted," answered Hurst-Brown.

"Thank you, Your Honor." Shadid went on the counterattack. "While the defense puts forth an interesting linguistic argument, it isn't consistent with the facts. The defense contends that the Iraq War was never intended to be 'a large-scale invasion.' That is in total contradiction to the facts. American-led coalition forces waged a full-scale war using massive military force that was described by many as 'shock and awe.' More than three hundred thousand troops were used, and the United States spent more than a billion dollars a day fighting that war. Anybody who knows the facts could only describe it as a large-scale invasion. As a result, Iraq was defeated within months—weeks, really.

"Next, the prosecution pleads that the Court reject the defense's use of Article 8(2), which states that civilian casualties are acceptable in light of the military advantage gained. War crimes, as defined in international law, are committed if the perpetrator is responsible for the killing of even one person. The defendant's war caused the deaths of more than a million and a half human beings, as reported in the respected British medical journal *The Lancet*.

"As to 'military advantage gained,' *what* military advantage was gained? World War II was fought to stop the spread of Hitler's Nazi regime in Russia and Europe. The Vietnam War was fought to address the Western world's fear of communism spreading in Asia—the 'domino theory,' as it was called. Iraq wasn't trying to spread its ideology, even if it had one. It was only trying to maintain its sovereignty in the contentious Middle East, which took constant diligence. Following the Gulf War that ended in 1991, containment, sanctions, and inspections had eliminated Saddam's ability to threaten other countries, most certainly including the United States.

"What the defense counsel refuses to take responsibility for is George W. Bush causing the war and recognizing the tremendous carnage in terms of military and civilian lives lost, and physical structures destroyed as a result of his war. Four years after the war started, on April 29, 2007, former CIA Director Tenet said in a primetime telecast on the CBS news program *60 Minutes,* 'We could never verify that there was any Iraqi authority, direction, control, or complicity with al Qaeda for 9/11.' Dr. Robert Leiken of the Nixon Center stated, 'Numerous post-9/11 inquiries together comprising probably the most comprehensive criminal investigation in history . . . chasing down five hundred thousand leads and interviewing one hundred and seventy-five thousand people . . . turned up no evidence of Iraq's involvement with al Qaeda, or the 9/11 attack.'

"George W. Bush's stated goals for waging his war were first to remove WMD, of which there were none. Then it was to protect America from an attack by Iraq. As has been proven, Saddam had no interest in attacking America, nor did he have the capacity to do so even if such an interest existed. As a reminder, Saddam Hussein was once an ally of the United States. In the early 1980s, Iran's shah was overthrown by the Ayatollah Khomeini, which led to the Iran-Iraq War. Saddam invaded Iran with the support of Arab states, Europe, and the United States, all of which provided funding and military equipment. Saddam was regarded as the defender of the Arab world. Nevertheless, with absolutely no justification for attacking Iraq and toppling Saddam, and all the justification in the world for finding and killing bin Laden and destroying al Qaeda, George Bush started his war with Iraq. Even his brother Jeb Bush, while campaigning for the presidency in 2015, said, 'Based on what we now know, I wouldn't have gone in. It was a mistake.'

"The facts prove that the defendant was repeatedly given relevant and accurate information, and yet he chose to ignore it. Considering the people he interacted with on a daily basis at the White House, it is impossible for him not to have known this information. The truth is that George W. Bush knew these facts during the entire buildup to the war and chose to ignore them because the truth did not serve his agenda. He spread false information that supported his war so he could gain the approval necessary to wage his war. Why didn't he just find and kill Osama bin Laden and thus satisfy America's public thirst for the revenge of 9/11? It should be noted that after Mr. Bush had left office, in May 2011, President Barack Obama ordered an attack in which sixteen Navy SEALs entered a house in Abbottabad, Pakistan, and in fifteen minutes found and killed Osama bin Laden, after which they departed with his body to bury at sea.

"There are, of course, other possible motivations for George W. Bush's war. A war would stimulate the US economy and satisfy his voter base—note that he easily won his second-term election. A war would protect Israel. A war would avenge the assassination attempt on his father. It would protect US allies' oil interest in Iraq and the region. The fact is we may never know why Mr. Bush waged his war, unless he decides to tell us. But wage his war he did, and now he must bear the responsibility for the consequences of that war.

"Your Honors, the prosecution would like to engage in a little housekeeping and address some applicable legal rudiments at this time," Shadid said, walking confidently toward the judges and seeming at the top of her game. "Article 30 of the Rome Statute provides that a person shall be criminally responsible and liable for punishment of a crime within the jurisdiction of the Court only if the material elements are committed with intent and knowledge. Existence of Mr. Bush's intent and knowledge are confirmed by actual facts. The prosecution has proven that the defendant had clear and abundant intent and knowledge before and during the Iraq War. Thank you, Your Honors. The prosecution rests."

"Thank you, Ms. Shadid. Does the defense counsel wish to refute the prosecution's assertions?"

"No, Your Honor," Ed White responded quickly. "We'll let the facts speak for themselves."

"Thank you, sir," Hurst-Brown said and rapped his gavel. "Court is adjourned until 9:00 AM tomorrow, at which time the prosecution may commence with witness testimony."

5

Parade of
Prosecution Witnesses

*"In a time of universal deceit, telling
the truth is a revolutionary act."*

—ANONYMOUS

THE USUAL ASSEMBLAGE WAS PRESENT IN THE ICC courtroom on the
following morning; the usual crowd was again watching on
the monitors outside. After Presiding Judge Hurst-Brown gaveled
the trial into session, co-prosecuting attorney Nadia Shadid began.

"Good morning, Your Honors. The prosecution would like to
state that it will present an abundance of witness testimony along
with multinational government statistics that prove beyond any
lingering doubt that hundreds of thousands of Iraqi, American,
British, Australian, Danish, Polish, and others were killed or seriously wounded in George W. Bush's war. To begin, we wish to call
the Court's attention to Prosecution Evidence #1."

Per standard courtroom procedure, the ICC judges, defense
team, and all others in the courtroom and public gallery looked at
the monitors or referred to the binders of evidence provided.

"This document, according to US military intelligence sources,
is a complete list of all American soldiers who lost their lives in
the Iraq War," Shadid continued. "Included are the name, picture,
hometown, military rank, age, and date of death of each of the

deceased. The list is presented in chronological order from the first American soldier to die, Jonathan Lee Gifford, age thirty, of Decatur, Illinois, who was killed in action on March 23, 2003, three days after the war began, to the last American soldier to die, David Emmanuel Hickman, age twenty-three, of Greensboro, North Carolina, who died on November 14, 2011.

"Your Honors, as mothers, fathers, wives, husbands, siblings, and friends of these fallen soldiers have had to relate and relive their emotional pain many times already, we will provide a measured amount of testimony regarding military deaths. Every bit as important as the American and Iraqi casualties suffered in the war is the experience of Iraqi citizens during the war. It is in this context, Your Honors, that I request permission to approach the bench."

Hurst-Brown granted permission, and Shadid approached the bench. Seeing this, co-defense attorney Meredith Lott approached the bench as well. The two opposing attorneys exchanged brief but hostile looks before Shadid spoke again.

"Your Honors, the prosecution's first witness is a woman from Iraq who became a somewhat famous blogger during the Iraq War. She has agreed to testify under the condition that her identity be kept secret, as she wishes to remain outside the public view for the safety and security of herself and her family. She is here at the ICC but will testify only if she can wear a burka, have her voice distorted, and use the name under which she published her blog. Her testimony is critical to the prosecution's case, and we plead for approval from the Court to proceed with this witness."

"Your Honors, we strongly object," Lott countered. "Our client has the right to know the identity of his accusers and to contest the evidence given against him. How can we do so if we don't even know her real identity and can't even see her face? Article 67 of the Rome Statute guarantees these rights in a fair trial."

"Maybe so," Shadid responded, "but Article 68 empowers the Court to protect witnesses who may be in danger of retaliation for cooperating with the Court. Keeping this witness's identity secret is critical to her safety."

"This is exactly why the ICC had black curtains installed over the public gallery windows," Lott countered again. "Just draw the curtains closed and disallow the burka. At least we'll be able to see who she is."

"Your Honors, please do not forget the overriding issue of transparency and public interest in this trial. If we close the curtains, the ICC will seem to be operating in secret, which will undermine its legitimacy as an institution. By letting our witness wear her burka, she remains concealed without the Court having to hide the trial from the world."

"But, Your Honors," Lott interjected, "our client's rights are more important than the public's right to view the trial."

After consulting sotto voce with her fellow judges, Judge Miyako Kimura informed the opposing attorneys of the Court's decision. "You both raise valid points. However, on balance, we believe that keeping this trial public and transparent supersedes the defense's need to see this witness's face and best serves the ends of justice. Ms. Shadid, if your witness refers to her blog posts, will you make them available to the Court?"

"Yes, Your Honors."

"Then permission is granted."

"Thank you, Your Honors."

Ms. Shadid, pleased and anxious to get started, and Ms. Lott, obviously perturbed with what had just happened, ignored each other and returned to their seats.

Prosecuting attorney Shadid called the first witness for the prosecution. A woman wearing a burka with a narrow slit only wide enough to reveal her eyes was led into the courtroom by UN guards. As the woman entered, she stopped, looked around the room, and settled her gaze on George Bush. No one spoke. The Iraqi woman continued staring at Bush until he looked away, and then proceeded to the witness bench and sat.

Shadid began by first addressing the judges. "Your Honors, as you no doubt know, there is a very important statement written on a wall in the lobby of this building which says volumes about the ICC. For those of you who do not know, it reads, 'True justice is achieved when voices of victims are heard and their suffering is addressed.' Here at the ICC, for the first time in the history of international criminal justice, victims have the right to participate in proceedings and request reparations. This means they may not only testify, but can also present their views and concerns. This woman contacted the prosecution and asked to testify. We were pleased to accept her offer."

Shadid turned back to the woman and smiled warmly. "Thank you for your bravery. Please know that your voice will be distorted here in the courtroom, on all public showings, and on all other recordings made of your testimony. First, to comply with ICC regulations, all witnesses must read the swearing-in document. Would you please do so now?"

"I solemnly declare that I will speak the truth, the whole truth, and nothing but the truth," the woman read softly into the microphone, the audio from which could be heard throughout the courtroom and the rest of the world.

"Thank you. The Court has agreed that we can refer to you as 'Riverbend,' the pen name you used for your blog," Shadid noted and began her questioning. "Other than your name, would you please introduce yourself?"

"I am female. I am Iraqi. I survived the war. That's all you need to know. That's all that matters."

"Why did you start writing your blog?"

"Because I became convinced that George Bush had determined to go to war against Saddam well before 9/11, even though all his claims about weapons of mass destruction were proven to be false, as most Iraqis knew they would be. George Bush's war was based on inaccurate and dishonest reasoning. After he declared 'mission accomplished' on May 2, 2003, one and a half months into the war, his war was no longer a war. At first, some Iraqis welcomed the American conquest. The occupation was initially awkward but then quickly became stupid and criminal. The United States never gained enough control to restore any sort of order. Regardless of the enthusiasm some Iraqis had for the war at its outset, the ongoing support and cooperation from coalition forces that was expected by Iraqis on the street never came."

Shadid prodded her gently. "Your first blog post went up on August 17, 2003, almost five months to the day after the US invasion."

"Yes. I wanted to start earlier but I thought, 'Who will read it?' Over time I figured I had nothing to lose. I warned people in my first blog post to expect a lot of complaining and ranting."

"And you have some of your blog posts with you?"

"Yes. As these events happened many years ago, I thought reading my blog would be better than speaking from memory."

"We know you experienced firsthand the death of many friends, friends of friends, and family. May we call your attention to your blog post of August 19, 2003, and would you please read from that entry?"

Riverbend flipped through her blog posts, came upon the correct one, and began to read.

"Today a child was killed. His name was Omar Jassim, and he was no more than ten years old, maybe eleven. Does anyone hear that? Do they show that on Fox News or CNN? He was killed during an American raid. No one knows why. His family is devastated. Nothing was taken from the house because nothing was found. But the truth is that the raids accomplish only one thing: They act as a constant reminder that we are under occupation. We are not free. We are not liberated. We are no longer safe in our homes. Everything now belongs to someone else. I can't see the future at this point, or maybe I choose not to see it. We're living in this moment with a future we are afraid to contemplate. It's like trying to find your way out of a nightmare. I just wish the Americans would take the oil and go."

Shadid phrased her questions with increasing urgency. "We move to the very next day. The UN headquarters in Baghdad is bombed. Twenty-two people are killed. Among the dead is UN Special Envoy Sergio de Mello, an able diplomat highly respected and regarded by both sides, and widely viewed as the one man who might be able to blend together the complex politics of war-torn Iraq. Would you please read from your blog post of August 20, 2003?"

Riverbend read the blog post. "Sergio de Mello's death was a catastrophe. In spite of the fact that the UN was futile in stopping the war, seeing someone like de Mello gave Iraqis some sort of weak hope. It gave you the feeling that no, Americans could not run amok in Baghdad without the watchful eye of the international community. America, as an occupying power, is responsible for the safety and security of what is left of this country. It has been shirking its duties horribly. But you would think with someone like Sergio de Mello, it would have gotten better. I'm terrified. If de Mello could not be kept safe, what's going to happen to the millions of people fearing for their lives in Iraq?"

Shadid allowed for a moment of quiet reflection and continued.

"On November 27, 2003, President George W. Bush paid a visit to Baghdad. It was the subject of one of your blog posts."

"Yes, he landed at Baghdad International Airport, but don't let the name fool you. It's about twenty miles outside of town. No one is allowed to go near the area. He was gone before any of us knew he had even arrived."

The Iraqi woman looked up from her writing, locked eyes with Bush, and spoke directly to him.

"Why did you do that? Why did you sneak in and out of Iraq with such secrecy? Why did you not walk the streets of the country you say you liberated?"

She stared intently at the former president for many seconds before he blinked and turned away. Then she continued reading from her blog post.

"Bush must be proud today; two more terrorists were shot dead. Actually the two 'terrorists' were sisters, one twelve years old and the other fifteen. They were shot by coalition troops while gathering wood from the field, but nobody bothered to report that. They are two Iraqi girls in their teens who were brutally killed by occupation troops—so what? Bush's covert two-hour visit to the Baghdad International Airport is infinitely more important."

Shadid pressed forward with more urgency. "On February 17, 2004, the *New York Times* published an article entitled 'Arabs in US Raising Money to Back Bush.' Would you read what you wrote that day?"

Riverbend took a moment to find the post.

"The article was written by Leslie Wayne," she said, "who knows very little about geography. It basically states that a substantial sum of money supporting Bush's presidential campaign is coming from affluent Arab-Americans who support the war on Iraq. Of the five prominent 'Arabs' the author gives as examples of Bush supporters, two are Iranian and a third is Pakistani. Now, this is highly amusing to an Arab, because Pakistanis aren't Arabs. And while Iran is our neighbor, Iranians are, generally speaking, not Arabs. You can confirm that with Iranian bloggers. I just wish all those prominent Americans who supported the war—you know, the ones living in Washington and London who attend state dinners at the White House—would pack their Louis Vuitton bags and bring all that money they are contributing to the 'war-hungry imbecile' in the White House instead to Iraq or Iran to spread democracy and help 'reconstruct' and 'develop' these countries."

"Would you please go to your blog posts of March 2004 and share some of them with us?" Shadid said.

Riverbend flipped through a few pages and then stopped.

"Events in the United States are not helping Bush," she read. "David Kay, whom the Bush administration confidently predicted would bring home proof of Saddam's weapons of mass destruction, instead tells a Senate committee he can't find any evidence of their existence, and that prewar intelligence was 'almost all wrong.' Did the United States get bad intelligence or did Bush manipulate the intelligence for his own ends? Meanwhile, the insurgency mounts. One hundred Iraqis died in suicide bombings in January. On February 10, fifty-four Iraqi people are killed in a bombing as they apply for work at a police station. The next day, forty-seven die in an attack outside the Army recruiting center. The insurgency spreads and becomes more intense. Attacks in Karbala kill over one hundred and wound over three hundred. In a car bombing of a Baghdad hotel, twenty-seven people are killed, forty-one wounded."

"March 20, 2003, was the first day of the war," Shadid stated, and then questioned, "one year later you posted on your blog?"

"Yes," Riverbend said and started to read again. "One year ago on this day, the war started during the early hours of the morning. Now, 365 days later, Baghdad has been reduced to rubble. Our electricity is intermittent at best. There are constant fuel shortages and the streets aren't safe. We are trying to fight against extremism that seems to be upon us like a black wave. We watch with disbelief as American troops roam the streets of our towns and cities and break into our homes. Our government facilities have been burnt to the ground. Fifty percent of the working population is jobless and hungry. The streets are dirty and overflowing with sewage. Our jails are fuller than ever with thousands of innocent people. We've seen more explosions, tanks, fighter planes, and troops in the last year than in almost a decade of war with Iran. Our homes are being raided and our cars stopped in the streets for inspections. Iraqi journalists are being murdered. Hospitals overflow with patients but are short on everything else: medical supplies, medicine, and doctors. And all the while oil is flowing."

Rereading her blogs made Riverbend angry all over again. She took a deep breath, exhaled slowly, and bowed her head. Noticing this and wanting to be sure her witness stayed on point, Nadia Shadid prodded her to continue. Riverbend looked up with tears in her eyes.

"From one Iraqi woman to another," Shadid persisted, "please read your blog post of April 9, 2004."

The witness gathered herself and continued.

"April 9, 2004; the day the Iraqi puppets called 'National Day' will be marked by us as the day of the Fallujah Massacre. Over three hundred are dead in Fallujah. They are buried in the town football field because no one is allowed near the cemetery. The bodies are decomposing in the heat, and the people are struggling to bury them as quickly as they can. The American statistics don't show the real number of dying Iraqis. They don't show the women and children wounded and bleeding. They don't show the hospitals overflowing with the dead and dying because they don't want to hurt the Americans' feelings."

Riverbend again directed her comments at Bush.

"But American people should have seen the human devastation. You, George Bush, you should have seen with your own eyes the price your war had on my people . . . my country."

Bush stared at the woman from Iraq blankly.

Shadid allowed the moment to register with the judges, who sat engrossed in the testimony.

"Thank you very much," she concluded. "We have no more questions. Would you like to say anything else?"

"Yes, I would. The American invasion and occupation of Iraq pushed my country into a civil war. A strong Sunni insurgency made security impossible in certain parts of the country. At the same time, Shia leaders with help from Iran pulled together the majority of Shia into a political coalition. With Americans unable to maintain security, it left Iraq disabled, defenseless, and vulnerable. We know what happened after that; Islamic extremists seized the opportunity to use Iraq as a training ground to fight Western influences."

For a final time, the Iraqi witness turned to address her hated enemy.

"In case anybody is still wondering how the Islamic State was born and why the renewed hatred of the West came about, you can trace it back to George W. Bush's war. He claimed he was making the world safer by invading Iraq. In the end, all he did was destroy Iraq and leave the world exposed to terrorism the likes of which it had never seen."

Bush seemed unmoved, dismissive. He glanced over at Ed White, who returned a look of quiet confidence.

"Thank you, Your Honors," Shadid said. "We have no further questions."

"Thank you, Ms. Shadid," Judge Kimura said, turning her attention to the defense. "Does defense counsel wish to cross-examine this witness?"

Meredith Lott stood. "Your Honor, we note for the record that the Court has not provided the defense preparatory information for this witness or offered us the opportunity to meet with her. And since you have decided to also violate your own Rome Statute by determining that the public's view of this trial is more important than our client's rights, we have only seen someone in a burka and cannot possibly gauge this witness's state of mind in order to correctly calibrate our cross-examination. Nonetheless, defense does wish to cross-examine."

"Ms. Lott, the Court notes your objections," Judge Kimura responded. "You may proceed."

"Thank you, Your Honor." Lott smiled at Riverbend and began. "Hello."

Riverbend responded only with an icy stare.

"We understand your pen name is Riverbend, but would you please state your actual name in full for the benefit of the Court's records?"

"My actual name is not of consequence. What is of consequence is the content of my message. It was agreed that I could testify under the name I used to write my blog, and that is the name I will use. I wish to remain anonymous so I may continue to write the truth about the residual effects the Iraq War is having on my country without fearing for my safety. I am an Iraqi citizen, a woman, and a Muslim. That should be sufficient."

"Okay, 'Riverbend,' we begin. The Muslim religion includes different sects. One's own personal allegiance could well affect one's view of the war, especially as it relates to Saddam Hussein, who was a Sunni Muslim."

"Don't blame the Muslim religion," Riverbend shot back. "Every religion has its extremists. In times of chaos and disorder, those extremists flourish. Iraq is full of moderate Muslims who simply believe in the concept 'live and let live.' We get along with each other—Sunnis and Shiites, Muslims, Christians, Jews—we intermarry, we mix and mingle, we live. We build our churches and mosques in the same areas. Our children go to the same schools. Religion was never an issue. Next question, if you have one."

"Your collection of blog posts was published in a book entitled *Baghdad Burning*, correct?"

"Yes."

"The title itself indicates your view of the war. You know better than I that many Iraqis welcomed that war because it meant the overthrow of Saddam."

"I can promise you fewer Iraqis welcomed that war than George Bush thought or wanted."

"Clearly you're anti-American."

"When I hear 'anti-American,' it angers me. Why does America always identify itself with its military and government? Why does being anti-Bush and anti-occupation have to mean a person is anti-American? I am on the side of humanity, freedom, and life, and that's what my book reflects."

"You say you're on the side of humanity, freedom, and life. Thousands of American and coalition soldiers fought and died to free the Iraqi people from the clutches of its evil dictator. Have you no compassion for those lives?"

"There was a time when Iraqi people felt sorry for the troops, regardless of their nationality. We would see them suffering under the Iraqi sun, obviously wishing they were somewhere else, and somehow that vulnerability made them seem less monstrous and more human. But that time passed. Two transitional moments included the destruction of Fallujah and then the notorious photographs of torture at Abu Ghraib prison."

"Thank you, Ms . . . whatever your name is," Lott said. Realizing she might be doing more damage than good with her cross-examination, she turned quickly to address the ICC judges. "Your Honors, the defense rests."

"Thank you, Ms. Lott," Judge Kimura said. Then, turning to Shadid, she asked, "Does the prosecution wish to redirect this witness?"

"No, thank you, Your Honor," Shadid answered with a sense of accomplishment.

"The Court would like to thank the witness from Iraq and wish her a safe journey home."

The woman stood, nodded slightly in the direction of the judges, and was escorted toward the exit by UN guards. As she walked, she purposefully ignored Bush. When she was gone, the former president lowered his gaze to the floor.

The prosecution called its next witness, Mr. Richard A. Clarke, who read the swearing-in document, after which Ms. Shadid began her questioning.

"Mr. Clarke, thank you for joining us today."

"My pleasure."

"Please state your full name."

"Richard Alan Clarke."

"Born in the United States?"

"Yes. Dorchester, Massachusetts."

"Educated in the United States?"

"Bachelor's degree from the University of Pennsylvania. Master's from the Massachusetts Institute of Technology, among other things."

"Isn't MIT considered one of America's finest institutions of learning?"

"Yes."

"As for your diplomatic career, you served under President Ronald Reagan as deputy assistant secretary of state?"

"Yes, for intelligence."

"During the administration of George H. W. Bush, you were assistant secretary of state for political-military affairs?"

"Yes."

"During the Clinton administration, you were counterterrorism coordinator for the National Security Council?"

"Yes."

"And when President George W. Bush took office, you went to work for him. What was your post?"

"National coordinator for security, infrastructure protection, and counterterrorism."

"And your responsibilities were?"

"All matters dealing with terrorism and counterterrorism."

"By the time you worked for George W. Bush, you had served seven presidents in a career spanning thirty years, correct?"

"Yes."

"Would it be accurate to say you were America's foremost authority on terrorism and counterterrorism at that time?"

"Certainly one of the most knowledgeable and experienced."

"George W. Bush was inaugurated on January 21, 2001. Only days after the inauguration, you requested an urgent meeting. Why?"

"Because we needed to discuss America's greatest threat at the time, al Qaeda and its leader, Osama bin Laden."

"Did your request mention anything about Saddam Hussein or Iraq?"

"No. At that time, we judged Saddam and Iraq to be of minimal risk."

"You requested an urgent meeting with the president to discuss America's greatest threat. What was Mr. Bush's response?"

"He refused to meet at that time."

"Surely he must've met with you soon thereafter?"

"No. No, he did not. And after that, all the memos I sent to the president were not delivered, but rather they were passed down the chain of command and ultimately bounced back to me."

"So, what happened?"

Clarke glanced over at Bush, took a deep breath, let it out, and smiled, apparently pleased to finally get the opportunity to tell his story in a court of law.

"Some members of Mr. Bush's national security team and others agreed to meet with me. But the meeting wasn't scheduled in January or February or even March. Obviously they didn't consider it urgent or important. Finally, in April, four months after Bush's inauguration and my request, a meeting with junior staff was convened in the Situation Room of the White House."

"Would you please tell us about this meeting?"

"I told them we needed to deal with the threat posed by al Qaeda. I said we needed to put pressure on both al Qaeda and the Taliban by arming the Northern Alliance and other groups in Afghanistan. Simultaneously, we needed to target bin Laden and his leadership team.

"Paul Wolfowitz, Mr. Bush's deputy secretary of defense, responded by saying, 'I just don't understand why you're beginning to talk about this one man, bin Laden.' I replied as clearly and forcefully as I could that we were talking about a network of terrorist organizations called al Qaeda, which was led by bin Laden, and that we were talking about this network because it and it alone posed the most immediate and serious threat to the United States. Wolfowitz said, 'There are others as well. Iraqi terrorism, for example.' I told him I was unaware of any Iraqi-sponsored terrorism directed at the United States since 1993, and that the CIA and FBI would concur with my judgment. CIA deputy director John McLaughlin agreed with me and added, 'We have no evidence of any active Iraqi terrorism threat against the United States.'"

Shadid prodded. "US intelligence agencies were telling George Bush and his closest advisors that al Qaeda and bin Laden were a threat, and the administration would not listen?"

"That is correct. They ignored our very clear warnings."

"However, Bush's closest advisors countered by bringing up the matter of Iraq and Saddam Hussein being a threat, even though there was no evidence to suggest he was a threat of any kind?"

"That is correct."

"Are you sure of that, Mr. Clarke?"

"In the intelligence business, there is no such thing as 'sure.' But based on all the evidence we had, both empirical and actual, yes, I can state that Saddam Hussein did not present a credible threat to the United States at that time."

Then Shadid asked in a slow, measured voice, "Do you have any reason to believe this information did not get to President Bush's senior advisors, and ultimately to President Bush?"

"Objection, Your Honors," White interjected. "Calls for speculation."

"Objection sustained," Judge Miyako Kimura concurred.

Shadid took another tack. "Mr. Clarke, from your perspective as President Bush's chief intelligence officer, how attentive was he to incoming intel?"

"Mr. Bush had no real interest in the complicated issues and analysis related to terrorism. Early on, we were told that he was not a big reader. On issues he did care about, he believed he already had the answers. I learned over time that Mr. Bush was informed of foreign policy by talking to a small group of advisors: Dick Cheney, Don Rumsfeld, Paul Wolfowitz, Douglas Feith. He didn't like to read complex counterterrorism policy and objectives."

"Mr. Clarke, most of us are pretty familiar with the Bush team except for Douglas Feith. Can you tell us something about him?"

"He was President Bush's undersecretary of defense for policy, and one of his closest advisors."

"Is it accurate to say that, given your experience, Bush ignored or dismissed the input from conventional intelligence sources and instead paid attention to the people in his inner circle, who were only giving him information he wanted to hear?"

"Yes."

"And in your opinion, was he doing this because he was seeking justification for his war?"

"Yes."

"And what were the consequences of that?"

"As a direct consequence of Mr. Bush's lack of interest in learning the truth about terrorism and terrorist groups, he ordered the invasion of Iraq, which posed no threat to the United States. It didn't have to be that way. Nowhere on the list of things the United States should've done after September 11 was invading Iraq. The things we should've been doing after September 11 required an enormous amount of attention and resources, but they were not available because George Bush and his people were obsessed with Iraq. As a result of Bush's war, we delivered to al Qaeda the greatest recruitment propaganda imaginable and made it difficult for other friendly Islamic governments to be seen working closely with us."

"Mr. Clarke, as you look back on Mr. Bush's refusal to deal with al Qaeda and bin Laden, and instead to pursue his obsession over Saddam Hussein, what were the results?"

"After 9/11, George Bush squandered an opportunity to eliminate al Qaeda in Afghanistan, and instead strengthened our enemies by going off on a completely unnecessary tangent, Iraq. I knew al Qaeda was growing stronger in part because of our own actions and inactions. Al Qaeda and the offspring of the Iraqi insurgency were, in many ways, a tougher opponent than the original threat we faced before September 11."

"As one of America's most knowledgeable and respected authorities on terrorism and counterterrorism, how do you think history will look upon George W. Bush's war?"

At this point, Edward White stood. "Objection! Mr. Clarke's opinion is totally irrelevant to these proceedings."

Judge Kimura sustained the objection, so Shadid rephrased the question.

"Mr. Clarke, the war crimes of which George Bush is accused include willfully causing great suffering or serious injury, extensive destruction of property not justified by military necessity, and depriving prisoners the right to a fair trial. Based on your informed observation, how did the Iraq War start, what were its consequences, and what role did George Bush play in it?"

Clarke seemed happy to respond. "George Bush, as president of the United States, failed to act on the very real threat from al Qaeda prior to September 11, despite repeated warnings. He harvested a political windfall after the 9/11 attacks to launch an unnecessary and costly war in Iraq that strengthened the radical anti-American Islamic terrorist movement worldwide. Before Mr. Bush invaded Iraq, America was seen as a respected superpower. As a result of his war, America is now seen as a super-bully. When the United States needs international support in the future, who will join us? Who will believe us? Unless America addresses these real problems, it will suffer again."

"Mr. Clarke, you participated in a CNN documentary entitled *Long Road to Hell: America in Iraq*, which first aired in the United States in October 2015. In it, you said, 'If it were not for the American invasion of Iraq and the subsequent disbanding of the Iraqi Army by the United States, there would be no ISIS.' You couldn't have been more definitive or unequivocal."

"No. No doubt about it. ISIS is a direct outgrowth of the American invasion of Iraq."

"Caused and ordered by the defendant?"

"Yes. As president of the United States and commander in chief, George W. Bush was responsible for causing the war to happen and then ordering it officially to start."

"Thank you very much, Mr. Clarke."

"Thank you for the opportunity to set the record straight."

Her mission accomplished, Nadia turned confidently to the ICC judges. "No further questions, Your Honors."

"Thank you, Ms. Shadid," replied Judge Bankole. "Defense counsel, you are now free to cross-examine."

For the first time in the proceedings, defense attorney Jonathan Ortloff addressed the Court.

"Thank you, Your Honor. Mr. Clarke, isn't it true you also worked for a Democratic president?"

"Yes. President Clinton."

"And isn't it true that Mr. Bush is a Republican?"

"Yes."

"And to which political party do you belong, Mr. Clarke?"

"I don't see how that's got anything to do . . ."

Ortloff interrupted. "You're a registered Democrat. Isn't it true that President Clinton made you the country's chief counterterrorism advisor on the National Security Council?"

"Yes."

"And that granted you cabinet-level access?"

"Yes."

"You liked having that access, didn't you, Mr. Clarke?"

Clarke did not respond.

"In Washington, DC, access is power, and power is the coin of the realm," Ortloff continued. "You had it, but then you lost it, didn't you, Mr. Clarke?"

"You mean when George Bush became president?"

"Yes."

"My position was redefined."

"You were demoted by President Bush, weren't you, Mr. Clarke?"

"I wouldn't say that."

"There is no other way to say it. Your cabinet-level access was taken away from you, and, as a result, you lost much of your influence, access, and power."

"Not necessarily."

"Did you not testify earlier that you couldn't even get a memo to the president once you were working in the Bush administration?"

McBride leapt to Mr. Clarke's defense. "Objection, Your Honors. Badgering the witness."

"Objection sustained," Judge Bankole agreed. "Mr. Ortloff, just ask your questions and refrain from editorializing."

"Yes, Your Honor." Ortloff turned quickly back to Clarke. "You were promoted by a fellow Democrat, Bill Clinton, and demoted by a Republican, George Bush? How did that make you feel, Mr. Clarke?"

"It wasn't about that. It was . . ."

"Isn't your appearance here today an attempt to get even with a president who disregarded your experience, dismissed your professionalism, and ignored your advice?"

McBride interrupted again. "Objection, Your Honors! Defense is trying to intimidate and demean the witness."

"Overruled," Judge Bankole said.

Undaunted, Clarke answered the question. "George Bush refused to listen to the majority of US intelligence officials, who knew what was going to happen before it happened."

"Really? What was the exact date of the 9/11 attacks?"

"You've got to be kidding. September 11, 2001."

"And tell us, when did the 9/11 hijackers enter the United States?"

"Various times throughout 2000."

"Correct—when you were in charge of counterterrorism. They arrived on your watch and you didn't know about it, or even that they began training in flight schools in early 2001. All of that happened under your oversight, Mr. Clarke. Seems to me you couldn't have been such a great counterterrorism czar."

"No one could've known about . . ."

Ortloff pivoted to the judges. "Your Honors, we ask you to see this testimony for what it is. This witness is seeking to gain revenge against the defendant who demoted him, and who did so justifiably. Mr. Clarke was incompetent and ineffective at his job."

"That's not true!" Clarke shouted. "There's no way anyone could've . . ."

"Order! Order in the Court!" Judge Bankole interjected forcefully.

The courtroom took thirty seconds to quiet down before Ortloff spoke.

"No further questions, Your Honor."

"Thank you, Mr. Ortloff," Judge Bankole said and turned to address McBride and Shadid. "Does the prosecution wish to redirect?"

"No, Your Honor," Shadid responded, "but we would like to call the Court's attention to the rude and disrespectful questioning by defense counsel of a highly respected American intelligence official."

"Your opinion is noted, Ms. Shadid." Judge Bankole said and turned to the witness. "Mr. Clarke, the Court wishes to thank you for your testimony. You are excused."

Clarke stood, glanced at Bush a final time, and marched out of the courtroom.

Following Richard Clarke's testimony, the judges asked the defense team if it would like to cross-examine. It did not.

The prosecution rested.

6

Heavy Artillery

"Lead me, follow me, or get out of my way."
—General George Patton

On the following morning, Judge Omolade Bankole invited the defense attorneys to call their first witness. Meredith Lott informed the Court that it would be former Army General Tommy Franks. All participants and observers were keen to hear General Franks' testimony. Questioning from defense attorney Lott began at a rapid-fire pace.

"General Franks, you served in the United States military for thirty-eight years, correct?"

"Yes, ma'am, 1965 to 2003."

"In Vietnam, you were an artillery officer?"

"Yes, ma'am."

"And you were wounded three times?"

"Yes, ma'am. Third time was not the charm for me."

"Thank goodness. And you were a senior officer in Operation Desert Storm, otherwise known as the Gulf or Kuwait War?"

"Yes, ma'am."

"Most of us know you were in charge of coalition forces during the Iraq War. What was your official title?"

"Commander in chief of United States Central Command, ma'am."

"You were the boss?"

"Military boss, yes, ma'am," he said, smiling. "I had lots of other bosses above me."

"Including George W. Bush?"

"Yes, ma'am. He was the man. President of the United States."

"I'd like to start with your last meeting with President Bush before the invasion, March 5, 2003."

"Okay."

"As commander in chief of US Central Command, what did you report to the president?"

"I reported that coalition ground, naval, air, and Special Operations forces in the region had grown rapidly and totaled two hundred and ninety-two thousand. Of these, approximately one hundred and seventy thousand were US soldiers and Marines assigned to the combined forces land command."

"What was your opinion of Mr. Bush at the time?"

"Excuse me?"

"Was he calm, in control, forceful, angry?"

"I found him to be very focused. He's a guy who knows how to have a good time, but he's also very focused and very smart when he needs to be."

"Is there anything else you would like to add regarding your last meeting with Mr. Bush?"

"Yes. I told him all key infrastructure improvements had been completed and the required force was in the theater."

"You had personally spoken with the leaders of many US allies in the region?"

"Yes, ma'am. I had phone conversations with leaders in Jordan, Yemen, Pakistan, and Turkey. I had visited coalition troops in Afghanistan."

"And what was the opinion of these countries regarding the war? Were they, for the most part, in support of the Iraq War?"

"Yes, ma'am, for all the obvious reasons. Saddam Hussein was a cruel tyrant to his people and a destabilizing influence. His behavior was so erratic and unpredictable that he was of great concern to other countries in the region, especially with regard to oil production and sales."

"General Franks, your last prewar conversation with President Bush occurred March 19, 2003, the evening before the war started?"

"Yes, ma'am. The president was with his senior advisors in the White House. I was on the other side of a video link at Prince Sultan Air Base in Saudi Arabia."

"What can you tell us about that meeting?"

"President Bush was with Vice President Dick Cheney, Secretary of State Colin Powell, and other members of his National Security Council. Once we said our hellos, the president quickly moved to the purpose of the meeting. He said, 'You've got the National Security Council here,' and asked me to give a current update of our war plans. I thought it was important to provide the commanders of the US Army, Navy, Air Force, and Marines a chance to speak directly with the president, so we went around the horn, starting with Lieutenant General T. Michael 'Buzz' Moseley of the United States Air Force, and then US Army Lieutenant General David McKiernan, Vice Admiral Tim Keating of the Navy, and finally Marine Commander lieutenant General Earl Hailston. President Bush asked if they were satisfied with the war plans, and each responded in the affirmative."

"So, would it be accurate to say that senior command of these military forces—Air Force, Army, Navy, and Marines—were ready and confident to move forward with the invasion?"

"Yes, ma'am. 100 percent ready and confident."

"And all agreed with the president's battle plan?"

"Yes, ma'am. The United States military is trained to execute war plans as directed by the commander in chief."

"Would you say that the group's consensus, that sense of unanimous agreement, also would have applied to all two hundred and ninety-two thousand troops in the region?"

"Yes, ma'am, or they wouldn't have been there."

Having gained positive ground, Lott began to deflect some of what she thought might be the prosecution's negative contentions. "Some called the invasion 'shock and awe.' Where did that come from?"

"The media called it that, ma'am. They reported that targets were hit, buildings were shaking, and explosions were bigger and louder than anyone had ever heard. Al Jazeera said, 'All Baghdad is on fire.'"

"But you were striking military targets only, correct?"

"Yes, ma'am. Per a decision made by the president and Secretary Rumsfeld, we left Iraq's electrical power grid untouched. It made sense operationally and strategically. The president specifically said, 'We're not going to destroy Iraq. We're going to liberate the country from Saddam Hussein's regime.' So in building our targets, we excluded power plants, transformer stations, and electrical pylons and lines. The plan to preserve Iraq's infrastructure outweighed any possible military tactical disadvantage."

"Most of us have our own opinion of the war. What is yours?"

Michael McBride interrupted. "Objection, Your Honors. Calls for personal opinion and speculation."

"Objection overruled," Judge Bankole said. "The witness can answer the question."

Franks nodded at the judge, glanced at George Bush, and answered the question.

"Thanks to the decisions America's leaders made, the people

of Afghanistan and Iraq are free today. And rogue states around the world have been served notice. We need not apologize for the successes. History will state that America's strategy for fighting terrorism was a good one, and that the execution of Operation Iraqi Freedom by our young men and women in uniform was unequaled in its excellence by anything in the annals of war. People on the hometown streets of America know the truth. Today, Saddam Hussein is gone. Coalition forces rebuilt or constructed thousands of schools and hospitals. Today, thanks largely to the coalition, Iraqi medical professionals and healthcare far surpass what was available during Saddam's reign."

Obviously pleased with the former general's testimony thus far, Lott probed for more.

"General Franks, it needs to be asked: One of President Bush's reasons for going to war was the threat of Iraq's possession and potential use of weapons of mass destruction. What were and are your thoughts about these WMD?"

"I am frequently asked what I found to be most surprising during my tenure in Iraq. Each time, I answer: the absence of WMD. We went to war with reasonable expectations that we would find those weapons. Now some say we were duped into believing they existed and that we were wrong to have toppled Saddam Hussein's regime and free Iraq. I do not agree. As we all know, David Kay was the weapons inspector who led the US-Iraq survey group. He told a Senate committee his view was that, based on the best evidence he had, Iraq did indeed have weapons of mass destruction. They were elaborately shielded by deception operations that continued during and even after the Iraq War."

"But there is no question that you took out Saddam Hussein."

"Yes, ma'am, no question. There was plenty of evidence that Saddam and his sons had slaughtered a minimum of two hundred and ninety thousand innocent Iraqi men, women, and children. I'm proud of the fact that a dictator who had used WMD to murder his own people will never have a chance to use them on Americans. Tens of thousands of average Americans I met after the war have convinced me that the majority of my fellow citizens understand the principles of that war and agree we did the right thing. I think it was eighteenth-century British philosopher Edmund Burke who said that the only thing necessary for the triumph of evil is for good men to do nothing."

Lott allowed Franks' powerful testimony to pervade the room before continuing. "General Franks, by any standard you are a good man, a great American. Is there anything else you would like to say?"

"Yes, ma'am. We were blessed in America with great leadership that evidenced character, moral courage, and a depth of resolve seldom seen. We see evidence today of a core value that, in my opinion, was dormant after 9/11 and before the Iraq War—patriotism, constant patriotism by those who now salute the flag and wave it proudly." Franks then dramatically pointed his finger at the defendant. "And that leadership was provided in large part by the very man who sits before you in this courtroom, former President George W. Bush. And I want to take this occasion to personally thank him for it."

That said, General Franks stood and offered a snappy salute to his commander in chief, who returned the gesture in kind.

Meredith Lott added an exclamation point. "Thank you, sir."

"Pleasure, ma'am."

Lott then turned to the ICC judges.

"No further questions, Your Honors."

"Thank you, Ms. Lott," Judge Bankole responded and then addressed the opposing attorneys. "Does the prosecution wish to cross-examine this witness?"

"Yes, Your Honor," McBride answered.

"Please proceed."

"Thank you, Your Honor." McBride turned to the witness and nodded. "General Franks, please know we have only one goal here, and it is to determine, to the greatest degree possible, the truth of what happened before and during the Iraq War."

"Yes, sir. The truth will set us free."

"Now, General Franks, I don't want to be disrespectful in any way, but I do want to determine what happened. You suggest that America was blessed. As a spiritual man, do you wish for God to bless all peoples of the world?"

"Of course."

"Jesus preached that we should love all people."

"Yes, sir."

"Would that include people in the United Kingdom and the rest of Europe?"

"Of course."

"People in the Middle East? After all, Jesus was born and lived in the Middle East."

"Yes."

"Do you wish for God to bestow his love on the people of Iraq?"

"Yes, of course."

"Thank you. So do I. Your first meeting with George Bush occurred December 28, 2001, at his ranch in Crawford, Texas, correct?"

"Yes, sir."

"Toward the end of that meeting, you referred to a chart labeled 'Overreaching Concept.' Do you remember what it said?"

"Yes. It said regime change and WMD removal were the working targets."

"And all in attendance agreed with these goals?"

"Yes."

"Did it ever occur to you, or to the group, that as Osama bin Laden and al Qaeda were responsible for the 9/11 attacks, logically they should have been the targets to find and bring to justice?"

"Yes, but I was not president of the United States."

"So even though George Bush knew bin Laden was hiding in the mountains of Afghanistan or Pakistan, he basically ignored him and turned his attention, and yours, to Saddam Hussein and Iraq."

"No, sir. Incorrect. President Bush was interested in bin Laden as well."

"But when you couldn't get bin Laden, in time Bush turned his attention more and more to Saddam Hussein and Iraq."

"Yes, in time."

"So in March 2003, you led coalition forces totaling two hundred and ninety-two thousand soldiers to remove Saddam and find and destroy his WMD?"

"Basically, yes."

"Basically, factually, and actually, yes. Putting aside Saddam and WMD for the moment, if your sole target had been to capture or kill Osama bin Laden, given all the assets you had available, what would that have taken?"

"That's a hypothetical question."

"I beg to differ; it's a straightforward question. What in terms of manpower and time would it have taken to get bin Laden?"

Franks studied McBride, trying to decide if he should answer the question or not. Finally, he said, "Well, significant funding, a couple months of planning, consistently good intel, a few dozen SEALs, and some luck."

"And the thirst the American people had for revenge after the 9/11 attacks would have been satisfied?"

"That is your theory, sir."

"Yes. A theory shared by most people."

"Objection, Your Honors," Edward White interjected. "Conjecture."

Judge Hurst-Brown sustained the objection.

McBride quickly moved on. "Moving back to WMD. While nobody is saying Saddam didn't have and use WMD in the 1980s and '90s, there was a huge question of whether he actually had WMD at the beginning of the twenty-first century."

"Yes, sir, that was a question."

"And yet no one had found evidence that Saddam had WMD. UN inspectors who had been given free rein in Iraq had certainly not found WMD. Can we agree that no hard, confirmed intelligence proved beyond any doubt that Saddam had WMD?"

"Yes."

"General Franks, for the record and with the eyes of all humankind on you, and your God watching over you, did you find even one weapon of mass destruction in Iraq?"

"Well, sir, I was surprised that WMD were not used against our troops. And I was surprised that we did not find stockpiles of such weapons in Iraq."

"We'll take that as a no. So, after all was said and done, no weapons of mass destruction were found?"

"That's correct."

"General Franks, you may be aware that Thomas E. Ricks, senior Pentagon correspondent for the *Washington Post*, wrote a very fine book about the Iraq War entitled *Fiasco*. In it, he refers to a period of time during the buildup to the war in 2002 when the Bush administration's view departed from that of the US intelligence community at large. Mr. Ricks cited a senior Pentagon analyst who said, and I am now quoting, 'There wasn't anyone in the intelligence community who was saying to Mr. Bush what Pentagon analyst Douglas Feith was saying to Mr. Bush.'

"I would also like to quote Marine General Gregory Newbold, the Joint Staff's operations director, who said, 'It was also my sense that they,' referring to the Bush administration, 'cherry picked obscure, unconfirmed information to reinforce their own philosophies.' So it is clear that President Bush had people like Douglas Feith at the Pentagon, and others in his administration, serving up intel they knew he wanted to hear."

Franks nodded reluctantly. "They were giving the president intel, that is correct."

"And isn't it true that much of it did not reflect what the great majority of US intelligence agencies were saying at the time?"

"I'm aware that there were contradictory views."

"Isn't it true, General Franks, that you referred to Douglas Feith as 'the dumbest fucking guy on the planet'? Did you say that, sir?"

"Yes."

"One of Douglas Feith's colleagues, retired Army Lieutenant Jay Garner also said of Feith, 'I think he's incredibly dangerous. He's a very smart guy whose electrons aren't connected.'"

"No comment."

"So the opinions of senior military officials, including yourself, were that one of Bush's most relied-upon sources of information was considered to be, and again these are not my words but the words of people who should know, 'the dumbest fucking guy on the planet' and 'incredibly dangerous'?"

Franks and McBride glared at each other until the prosecuting attorney continued.

"General Franks, you probably know only too well that the official count of US soldiers killed in Iraq is said to be forty-five hundred. In addition, tens of thousands of American soldiers were wounded physically, mentally, or both. Many of them are still suffering today."

"Yes."

"Do you know how many Iraqi soldiers were killed in that war?"

"I believe approximately twenty thousand."

"Yes. And the number of Iraqi civilians killed?"

"I do not have that information."

"That's to be expected because it's a difficult number to determine. It is estimated to be more than half a million. Putting aside the cost in human lives, the war cost the United States more than four trillion dollars. Deep down in your heart of hearts, General Franks, was that war necessary?"

Ed White stood. "Objection, Your Honors. Calls for speculation."

Judge Bankole agreed. "Objection sustained."

"Mr. Franks, do you believe military commanders should exercise their own personal judgment of right and wrong when given orders by their superiors?" McBride quickly continued.

"It depends."

"On what?"

"A wide range of variables."

"If your commander in chief had asked you to cut the heads off all enemy combatants and rape all the women, would you have done these things, sir?"

"That's another hypothetical question, and a ridiculous one."

"Hypothetical, yes. But it's about as ridiculous as George Bush sending you to fight a war with massive military strength to do something that did not need to be done. That war had nothing to do with Saddam being a threat, or WMD, and he knew it."

"That may be your view, but it's not mine, and it's not the view of most Americans I know."

"Then you don't know many Americans. More than 60 percent of Americans opposed that war." McBride pivoted to another subject. "How familiar are you with the prisoner abuses at the Abu Ghraib prison facility?"

"It was a shameful chapter in the history of the United States."

"Care to elaborate?"

"Those outrages can never be excused. Millions of men and women have worn the uniforms of America's military with honor and compassion. As has been said so often, it only takes a few to smear the reputation of all. Unfortunate, but true."

"General Franks, I realize a great military leader such as yourself must remain steadfastly loyal to your commanding officers, certainly including the president of the United States. But I ask you, as you look back on the Iraq War, what are your personal thoughts?"

Franks looked over at Bush, wondering how much to say, how far to go. Bush sat motionless, staring back, presumably contemplating the same.

"I did not agree with every decision made before and during that war," Franks answered in a quiet, measured voice. "Many say President Bush should be blamed. I do not. I'm constantly amazed at the shallow thinking that underpins that opinion. Things go wrong in war. If war were easy and convenient, there would be too many of them."

McBride pushed for more. "No regrets?"

"Sure. I wish some things had been done differently. I wish the international community had infused more money into Iraq more quickly, and that Iraq's military hadn't melted away as our troops moved on Baghdad. I wish these young Iraqi men had committed themselves to building a new Iraq."

Sensing Franks might want or need to say more, McBride said nothing. Sure enough, after a long pause, the former commander of US Central Command in Iraq cleared his throat and continued.

"In the difficult days after the war, some asked me to lay blame—to point to guilty parties or condemn perceived misdeeds. I have said and will continue to say this: There's enough blame to go around. We live in a democratic society, a free country. We elect our leaders for their proven judgment, and we expect them to use that judgment for the common good."

"Thank you, General Franks. On a personal note, I hope you do not personally bear any shame or regret over that war. You only did what you were ordered to do by your commander in chief." McBride turned to the bench. "No further questions, Your Honors. Prosecution rests."

"Thank you, Mr. McBride," Judge Bankole said. "Does the defense wish to redirect?"

"Yes, Your Honor," White answered. "Just one thing more. General Franks, did you believe you were in command of this war, or did you feel you had to get approval from the White House for your operations?"

"You mean like General Westmoreland going back to President Johnson every week during the Vietnam War and asking for permission to do this or that? No. President Bush made it clear that he trusted his commanders to do the right thing, and that they would not be second-guessed by him."

"So you felt you were totally in control of this war?"

"Yes, sir."

"Thank you, General Franks. Nothing further."

"Thank you, Mr. White," Judge Bankole replied and turned again to the prosecutors. "Does the prosecution wish to re-cross-examine this witness?"

"Yes, Your Honor," McBride answered.

"Please proceed."

"General Franks, on your reading of the US Constitution, who is ultimately in charge of the armed forces?"

"Well, that would be the president."

"That's why they also refer to him as the commander in chief. He is literally at the top of the command chain, correct?"

"That's right."

"And George Bush knew what was happening in Iraq through his daily and sometimes even hourly briefings from you, the Defense Department, and the intelligence community?"

"As we covered before, yes."

"So he could've stopped all military operations at any time?"

"Yes."

"General Franks, I would appreciate an answer to this question, which has been bothering me for a long time. The Iraq War started in March 2003. In one month's time, Baghdad fell and Saddam's statue was toppled to the ground. In July, four months after the war had started, you left Iraq. For all intents and purposes, wasn't the war over by then? Why, after your forces had brought Iraq to its knees in a matter of months, did the war continue for a subsequent eight years? Why didn't America just go over there, do what it thought it had to do, and get the hell out?"

"You'll have to ask someone other than me. Higher powers."

"Thank you, General Franks." McBride turned to the judges. "Nothing further, Your Honors."

"Does the defense wish to redirect?" Judge Hurst-Brown asked.

"No, Your Honor," White responded. "Defense wishes to thank General Tommy Franks for his testimony and call its next witness."

"The Court thanks the witness for his testimony and wishes him a safe journey home. Defense may proceed with its next witness."

"Thank you, Your Honor," Edward White replied. "The defense calls Dr. Condoleezza Rice to the witness stand."

7
Quid Pro Quo

"Be with a leader when he is right, stay with him when he is still right, but leave him when he is wrong."
—ABRAHAM LINCOLN

LOOKING FOR WAYS TO FEED THE INSATIABLE public thirst for all things related to the trial, news organizations began to take polls to determine public opinion regarding the status of the case. Nowhere was this more apparent than in the United States.

Not surprisingly, when taken as a whole, the results of polls across all fifty states mirrored typical outcomes of presidential elections. States that customarily voted Republican, such as Alabama, Utah, and Oklahoma, polled in favor of Mr. Bush's innocence. States that customarily voted Democratic, such as New York, Illinois, and California, favored a guilty verdict. Swing states, such as Florida, Ohio, and Colorado, in which voting often depended on the subject matter of the time, were divided. Allowing for the customary statistical variants, a slightly larger cross-section of the American people thought Bush would be found not guilty. But then again, that could change with the testimony of the next witnesses and whether or not George Bush himself would testify.

Condoleezza Rice was born in Birmingham, Alabama, in 1954, the only child of a mother who was a high school science and music teacher, and a father who was a high school guidance counselor and Presbyterian minister. She was unmarried and had no children. She was America's first black female national security advisor and its first African-American secretary of state. Her given name drew its origin from the music-related term *con dolcezza* ("with sweetness" in Italian). She served George W. Bush as chief foreign policy advisor in his 2000 presidential campaign and left a prestigious appointment at Stanford University to join his administration when he was elected. Dr. Rice was a close friend and confidante of George Bush during his eight years as president—some say his closest.

Dressed in a natty suit and exuding supreme confidence, Dr. Rice entered the courtroom, read the swearing-in document, and took her seat on the witness stand. Lead defense attorney Ed White began.

"Greetings, Dr. Rice, and thank you for coming," he said.

"I regard it as my duty to be here," she answered.

"Dr. Rice, you served under George W. Bush during his entire presidency. In his first term, 2001 to 2004, you were his national security advisor, and in his second term, 2005 to 2008, you were secretary of state, correct?"

"Yes."

"Would it be accurate to say that during the span of his eight years in office, no one was in such close communication with the president as you were?"

"Yes."

"And you are fully aware of what this proceeding is about?"

"Yes, I am."

"As we speak here today, years after the Iraq War, would you please put into context the challenges President Bush faced as they related to Saddam Hussein and Iraq?"

Dr. Rice glanced over at her dear friend and former boss, and launched into her testimony like a professor lecturing graduate students at Stanford.

"It is easy to forget now, with all the attendant controversy surrounding the Iraq War, but concerns had been growing for a decade, which were shared by the international community and both sides of the aisle in the United States Congress, about Saddam Hussein's Iraq and its possible reemergence as a major threat to the Middle East. The air strike on Iraq that President Clinton ordered in December 1998 garnered a House vote of four hundred seventeen to five, resolving that the United States should support efforts to remove Saddam and promote the emergence of a democratic government."

Pleased with his star witness, Ed White framed his next question appropriately.

"So any president charged with protecting and defending the best interests of the American people would have had grave concerns about Saddam Hussein, especially when considering his propensity to build and use the most destructive weaponry known to man?"

"Exactly. After the 9/11 attacks, President Bush made it clear that the immediate problem was the al Qaeda sanctuary in Afghanistan. But in the spring of 2002, upon examining Iraq's WMD threat and its nexus with terrorism, the question of what to do about Saddam, who had a record of using chemical weapons against Iranian targets and ethnic minorities within his own population, was on the table again."

"And this concern was supported by intelligence officials reporting to the president?"

"Essentially, yes. The process of providing intelligence estimates is an imprecise science at best. At the time of the Iraq War, the United States had twelve intelligence agencies that tried to produce a joint assessment known as a National Intelligence Estimate, or NIE. Understandably, there are almost always differences of opinion among these agencies. President Bush, from the time he had taken office, had received increasingly alarming reports almost daily about Saddam's progress in reconstituting his WMD program. In October 2002, the NIE informed us that Iraq had continued its weapons of mass destruction program in defiance of UN resolutions. Saddam had chemical and biological weapons, as well as missiles with ranges in excess of UN restrictions. If left unchecked, Iraq probably would have a nuclear weapon within a few years."

White seized the opening provided by Dr. Rice.

"Yes, thank you for bringing up the NIE. While the prosecution has presented its slanted evidence of US intelligence, defense wishes to introduce the NIE report as Defense Evidence #1."

Meredith Lott delivered the document to the Court as White continued.

"Dr. Rice," White said, "I would like to read one of many sections from the NIE that forecasted great danger: 'We judge that all key aspects: R&D, production, and weaponization of Iraq's offensive biological weapons program are active and that most elements are larger and more advanced than they were before the Gulf War.'"

"Yes," Dr. Rice commented, and then quickly added, "it also stated that Baghdad had mobile facilities for producing bacterial and toxic biological warfare agents."

"We must all keep in mind that during the aftermath of 9/11, America and all peaceful nations were consumed with the new threat of terrorists and terrorism."

"Correct. Saddam was a known supporter of terrorism. He

paid families of Palestinian suicide bombers twenty-five thousand dollars apiece after every successful attack. He had harbored numerous known terrorists over the years. In the shadow of 9/11, the possibility that Saddam might arm terrorists with chemical or biological weapons, or even a nuclear device, and set them loose against the United States was very real to us. We failed to connect the dots before the 9/11 attacks and had never imagined the use of civilian airliners as missiles against the World Trade Center or the Pentagon. The thought that an unconstrained Saddam Hussein might aid terrorists in an attack on the United States did not seem far-fetched to us."

White was visibly pleased. Needing to counter the effect of the prosecution's witness testimony and build preemptive momentum for the defense, White pressed down harder on the accelerator.

"And given Saddam's history, it was highly unlikely he would succumb to any threat posed by the United States or other countries. Nonetheless, the Bush administration sought to use international pressure before resorting to war?"

"Yes. No one believed that Saddam would give up power peacefully. We were down to two options if we wanted to change course: Increase international pressure to make him give up his WMD, or overthrow him by force."

"And what was President Bush's view of all this?"

"The question of how to remove Saddam short of war was constantly on his mind," Dr. Rice said without hesitation. "We reached out to Arab leaders, asking them to assure Saddam that the United States would indeed overthrow him if he didn't comply with UN-mandated sanctions. The Egyptians claimed that Saddam's sons, Uday and Qusay, had sent a message that he would leave Iraq in exchange for one billion dollars. President Bush sent word that he would gladly pay. Nothing came of it."

"And given Saddam's well-known disdain and disregard for international pressure, America was confronted with the possibility of having to use force?"

"At the beginning of 2003, I was convinced we would have to use military force. Saddam seemed to be playing games with the UN and US inspectors, refusing interviews with his scientists, sending 'minders' along with them for meetings with inspectors. That is what passed for cooperation, and it seemed to be producing minimal information. Nonetheless, the inspectors, despite limitations, gathered evidence that Iraqi officials were moving various items and hiding them at suspect sites prior to inspection visits. The Iraqi dictator seemed to be up to his old tricks. Frankly, I couldn't understand it. Maybe he just didn't believe us."

"So it would be your opinion that Saddam Hussein posed the greatest threat to world peace at the time in question?"

"Yes. Saddam Hussein was a cancer in the Middle East who had attacked his neighbors and thrown the region into chaos. He had drawn the United States into conflict twice—once to expel him from Kuwait, and a second time to deliver air strikes against suspected WMD sites because he would not allow arms inspectors to do their jobs. Saddam was routinely shooting at our aircraft patrolling under UN authority. The UN sanctions put into place to contain him had crumbled under the weight of international corruption and his considerable guile. He had tried to assassinate a former president of the United States, and he supported terrorists—harboring some of the most notorious in his country. There had been no arms inspection in Iraq for more than four years. A majority of agencies within the US intelligence community believed he had reconstituted his nuclear weapons capability, and could possibly have a crude nuclear device within a year. Similar views were shared by many foreign intelligence organizations. The world had given Saddam one last chance to come clean about his weapons program or face serious consequences. This time, the word of the international community had to mean something."

"To those who engage the precious wisdom of twenty-twenty hindsight and contend that the Iraq War was a needless war, what would you say?"

"Nonsense. Prime Minister Tony Blair convinced the House of Commons to commit British forces to overthrow Saddam and liberate Iraq. Prime Ministers Howard of Australia and Kwaśniewski of Poland did the same. Eighteen NATO members and several other states joined the coalition. In fact, thirty-three countries provided troops to support our military operations in Iraq."

"Obviously, President Bush believed he had ample justification and validation for this war from the perspectives of both national and international law."

"Yes, and it was a logical assumption. The United States had long maintained the option of preemptive action to counter threats to its national security. And international law has for centuries recognized that nations need not suffer an attack before taking action against an imminent threat. In an age when enemies of civilized countries openly and actively seek to use the world's most destructive technologies, the United States could not remain idle while danger gathered. These enemies were of a different character than in the past—when threats had come largely from states in which there was some reasonable expectation that military preparation for an attack would be visible. Terrorists today operate in the shadows and can attack without warning, as they did on September 11. In light of this threat, limiting preemption only to those occasions when we were absolutely certain an enemy was about to attack made little sense."

"From your front-row seat during all this activity, as national security advisor and then secretary of state, were you 100 percent behind President Bush's decision to wage war against Iraq?"

"Yes, 100 percent."

"Thank you. Is there anything else you would like to add for the record?"

"Yes, thank you. Having spent my adult life in the study and teaching of political science, and from my knowledge of international criminal law, I would like to state categorically that this case brought by the International Criminal Court against Mr. Bush is disrespectful, reprehensible, and wholly uncalled for. I caution the ICC that it has acted carelessly and is overstepping its authority. The worldwide opinion of this Court should be seriously reconsidered as a result. This Court's very existence, I believe, is on trial here as much as George W. Bush is."

Dr. Rice's authoritative and confident testimony went a long way to validate George W. Bush and invalidate the trial itself. Ed White, looking like a proud father whose daughter had just graduated first in her class, warmly acknowledged his prized witness.

"Thank you, Dr. Rice, for setting the record straight," White said. Turning to face the judges, he concluded, "No further questions, Your Honors."

"Thank you, Mr. White," Judge Hurst-Brown said. "Does the prosecution wish to cross-examine?"

"Yes, Your Honor, we do," Ms. Shadid responded.

"Please proceed."

There had been a debate between Michael and Nadia regarding which of the two should take the testimony of Dr. Rice. For starters, both wanted to accept the maximum amount of personal responsibility in any contest to ensure victory over defeat. In the end, they concluded that Nadia, as an Iraqi woman, should have the honor and immense challenge of questioning the former secretary of state.

Nadia Shadid did not start with any sort of welcoming smile, as she knew Dr. Rice would only see it as patronizing, but rather simply said, "Dr. Rice, the prosecution also wishes to thank you for coming to testify at this tribunal. For those who may not know, and as inconceivable as it may seem, the ICC cannot itself subpoena or otherwise force a witness to testify. Witnesses appear in accordance with their own free will. So again, we thank you."

"As stated earlier," Rice snapped back, "I think it is my duty to testify on behalf of former President Bush. But my appearance here today in no way endorses what the ICC is doing, nor should it be understood to legitimize these proceedings in any way."

Shadid ignored the condescending rebuke and went to work.

"Dr. Rice, would you agree that the 9/11 attacks were masterminded and executed by al Qaeda, whose leader was Osama bin Laden, without any involvement of Saddam Hussein?"

"There was debate over the question of whether Saddam had played a role in the September 11 attacks. Some suggested that Saddam and al Qaeda were likely allies. I was never convinced by that argument."

"Thank you. America is a proud and powerful country. It is rightfully considered the leader of the free world. Would you agree that America had all the justification necessary to hunt down and destroy al Qaeda after the crimes they committed on 9/11?"

"Yes."

"Do you realize that in the entirety of your testimony for the defense, al Qaeda was mentioned only once, and Osama bin Laden was never mentioned?"

"No, but okay." Dr. Rice paused, knowing the question could be a trap. "The 9/11 attacks began at 8:46 AM Eastern Daylight Time.

The first statement from President Bush came at 1:04 PM. After asking for prayers for those killed or wounded, he stated that the United States would hunt down and punish those responsible for the cowardly acts. On the morning of September 12, the president held an intelligence briefing, which for the first time included the FBI director and the attorney general. Having not anticipated the attacks of 9/11, the intelligence agencies were determined not to be wrong again. CIA director George Tenet briefed us on the evidence of al Qaeda's complicity in the attacks. The president listened to the case against al Qaeda, and informed the War Council that we had crossed the threshold and would destroy the terrorists. The president's instructions were clear: Prepare to go to war against al Qaeda in a meaningful way, including the destruction of its safe haven in Afghanistan."

"And what about Osama bin Laden?"

"When his Saudi Arabian citizenship was revoked, bin Laden returned to Afghanistan where he built a base of operations for his terrorist network. The Taliban, sharing some ideological kinship with bin Laden, supported his efforts to establish al Qaeda training camps in Afghanistan. The immediate problem we faced after 9/11 was to defeat the Taliban and ultimately destroy al Qaeda."

"How and when did the focus shift from al Qaeda to Iraq and Saddam?"

"In a meeting on September 12, after some debate about how to proceed, Secretary of Defense Rumsfeld turned the floor over to his deputy, Paul Wolfowitz, who started talking about Iraq and focusing on the relative strategic importance of Iraq over Afghanistan. He suggested that a war in Afghanistan would be much more complicated than a straightforward engagement against a real army such as Saddam's in Iraq. It was awkward because everyone had come to the meeting thinking that the war would be fought in

Afghanistan. Honestly, I remember thinking Wolfowitz's comment was a huge distraction when there was so much to be done."

"Then what?"

"The president asked each member of his War Council for recommendations. Colin Powell suggested that the Taliban be given an ultimatum. He also stated that he was fundamentally opposed to action in Iraq. The president then turned to Vice President Cheney, who affirmed the war option and the need for an ultimatum. The president ended the meeting by confirming that this time al Qaeda must be defeated."

"So your recollection is that Deputy Secretary of Defense Wolfowitz first mentioned the need to focus on Saddam and Iraq, thus shifting the discussion away from al Qaeda and bin Laden?"

Rice, not wanting to be pandered to, responded, "Yes, as I said."

"What happened next?" Shadid pressed.

"The president asked for, and Congress passed, a resolution authorizing the use of military force on September 14, three days after the 9/11 attacks. This unified the country and the government's resolve to go after al Qaeda. On October 7, the president went before the American public to announce Operation Enduring Freedom. The United States was going to invade Afghanistan because the Taliban had refused to meet our demands to surrender al Qaeda's leaders and close terrorist training camps. It was President Bush's decision not to fight a big ground war but to rely instead on Afghan fighters, US Special Forces, intelligence, and air power."

"And the results of that strategy?"

"The initial phases of the plan were frustrating. US planes bombed the few installations that could be hit from the air. However, because Afghanistan's terrain was so rugged, mountainous, rural, and underdeveloped, the military quickly ran out of targets. When it was time to begin the ground assault, our 'cavalry' wasn't moving—saying they needed more equipment and better intelligence. George Tenet asked, 'Why don't they have the intelligence they need?' The answer was that the intelligence would come as they began to move forward and engage the Taliban forces. Growing impatient, the president complained, 'They just need to *move.*' The absence of action on the ground for days led to news coverage that trumpeted the 'quagmire' into which US forces had fallen."

"So, to be clear: President Bush did not wage a full-scale invasion in Afghanistan to find and destroy the perpetrators of the 9/11 attacks, but instead relied on Afghan fighters, US Special Forces, intelligence, and air power?"

"That's correct."

"One would think the president would use the full force of the US military to bring justice to those who committed the crimes of 9/11."

"The president obviously thought his was the best strategy, and he was the commander in chief."

"And when his strategy stalled, when he was not successful in either destroying al Qaeda or killing bin Laden, George Bush started to focus on Iraq and Saddam, correct?

"Eventually, he turned his attention to Iraq."

Seizing the opportunity to attack, Shadid posed the following question in a slow, clear, and definitive voice.

"The logical question then is: Why Saddam? When he had absolutely nothing to do with the 9/11 attacks and hadn't been an enemy of the United States for more than a decade, why Saddam?"

Dr. Rice responded quickly and confidently. "It was well understood at the time that Iraq was systematically violating the ceasefire agreement that it had signed in 1991 and evading UN sanctions that had been levied against it. Periodic crises had flared up in intervening years, leading arms inspectors to leave Iraq in 1998, allowing Saddam's WMD program to go unmonitored. When President Bush took office in January 2001, that was the situation we inherited and tried to address by strengthening the containment of Saddam's regime."

"And were those efforts successful?"

"Those efforts were frustrating and largely unsuccessful."

"Thank you for your candor, Dr. Rice. During your testimony to the defense, you referred to President Clinton's bombing of Iraq in 1998. That was three years before the 9/11 attacks, and five years before the US invasion of Iraq in 2003. It's all too clear that much can happen in one year, let alone over the course of five years! What exactly was Saddam Hussein doing in 2002, and leading up to the day of the invasion in March 2003, to make him and Iraq a 'clear and present danger' to the United States?"

Dr. Rice paused to consider her response.

"Iraq was on President Bush's mind. He was wondering how to use the threat of force to compel Saddam to comply with his obligations and destroy his suspected WMD."

Knowing she had Rice on the ropes, Shadid turned up the heat.

"You used the word 'suspected' because no one knew for certain that Saddam had WMD."

"Intelligence analysis of such covert activities is the art, not the science of piecing together information and drawing a picture of what is transpiring."

This was a crucial moment in Dr. Rice's testimony, as she herself had introduced the concept that intelligence gathering and reporting were often not as much about the facts as about speculation—the inference being, how could her former boss George Bush take his country to war on intelligence that was considered to be more speculative than factual? Shadid seized the opening and attacked with renewed vigor.

"Okay, Dr. Rice, let's talk about that. You mentioned in your testimony that at the time in question the United States had many separate intelligence agencies providing estimates of Iraq's capabilities, and that those agencies often disagreed in their assessments."

"Yes."

"Isn't it true that the National Intelligence Estimate that was mentioned, known as the NIE, included the findings of both the Bureau of Intelligence and Research and the intelligence arm of the US State Department?"

"Yes."

"And isn't it true that this bureau, known as the INR, had more than three hundred employees and a sixty million-dollar annual budget?"

"Yes."

Shadid turned to the ICC judges to introduce additional prosecutorial evidence as McBride handed a new document to the clerk.

"Your Honors, the prosecution wishes to submit Prosecution Evidence #2, the entire US State Department's INR report regarding its assessment of Saddam Hussein and Iraq at the time in question. With the permission of the Court, we wish to read a portion of the report into the record."

Hurst-Brown put his hand over the microphone in front of him, conferred in hushed tones with the other judges, and then announced to the Court, "Permission granted."

"Thank you, Your Honors. Quoting from the State Department's INR report: 'The activities we detected do not add up to a compelling case that Iraq is currently pursuing an integrated and comprehensive approach to acquire nuclear weapons. Iraq may be doing so, but INR considers the available evidence inadequate to support such a judgment. Lacking persuasive evidence that Baghdad has launched a coherent effort to reconstitute its nuclear weapons program, the INR is unwilling to speculate that such an effort began soon after the departure of UN inspectors, or to project a timeline for the completion of these activities.'"

Shadid turned back to the witness. "Dr. Rice, can you confirm that President Bush was given this intelligence report?"

"All available intelligence information was given to the president."

"And thus, we assume he got it and looked at it?"

"I assume nothing."

"Dr. Rice, true or false, US intelligence agencies were inconsistent and conflicted with regard to Iraq's possession of WMD."

Rice stared at Shadid for an awkward moment before stating in a measured voice, "This is a matter of public record; there were inconsistencies in the intelligence reporting, and no one could be sure what Saddam had."

With that concession from Dr. Rice, an eerie hush fell over the Court, as it was clear to all what a defining moment it was in the case. As Nadia Shadid had been a teenager when Bush had waged his war on her country, she had waited a long time to get a high-ranking US government official on the record regarding this subject. She paused long enough to let the significance of the moment register with the judges, and then transitioned to a new line of questioning.

"Thank you, Dr. Rice. Both you and defense counsel speak of 'imminent threat' when attempting to justify the Iraq War. Incontrovertible evidence proves that Saddam Hussein posed no threat to the United States in March 2003. The Iraq War started in

March 2003 and lasted until December 2011, eight years and nine months. It was a war that devastated the country and created a lawless territory into which revolutionaries and terrorists coalesced to create a rogue military force, which became known as the Islamic State. We are all aware of the devastation the Islamic State has caused, and continues to cause.

"Dr. Rice, the prosecution in this case has proven beyond any doubt that the defendant, George W. Bush, as president of the United States and commander in chief, is the person most responsible for causing this war. Under oath and for the millions of people who are now hearing or will hear your testimony, please tell us why this war happened."

The two women glared at each other while Rice considered her answer.

"UN-mandated sanctions were not working, the weapons inspections were unsatisfactory, and we could not get Saddam to leave by any other means," Rice replied.

"Dr. Rice, you are one of the most knowledgeable experts in the world on international law, and thus know that those reasons are not legal justifications for war. Again, was there any legitimate reason for that war?"

"We were trying to preempt Saddam and Iraq from any aggression against the United States or her allies, and felt a sense of urgency driven by the fact that our military forces were approaching levels of mobilization that could not be sustained much longer. A decision had to be made to either keep moving forward with the mobilization in Afghanistan or start pulling back. It wasn't possible to just stand still, since doing so would leave our forces vulnerable in theater without sufficient logistical support. The fact is that we invaded Iraq because we believed we had run out of other options.

We did not go to Iraq to bring democracy any more than Roosevelt went to war against Hitler to democratize Germany. We went to war because we saw Saddam Hussein as a threat to our national security and the security of our allies. The president did not want to go to war. We had come to the conclusion that it was time to deal with Saddam and believed that the world would be better off without him in power."

"Again, Dr. Rice, you know none of that is legal justification for war."

"Please do not be condescending to me, Ms. Shadid."

Ignoring Rice's rebuke, Shadid pressed on with her agenda. "Clearly, George Bush was getting conflicting information and advice from his vice president, secretaries, intelligence sources, and military advisors. But isn't it true, Dr. Rice, that the president relied mostly on his own counsel?"

"He listens to lots of people, and even prays over hard decisions. But in the end, he comes to his own decision— and sticks to it no matter what."

"Yes, exactly. His was the final decision. He was 'the decider.' That is why he is sitting here before the ICC today," Shadid pronounced. Then, sensing that the time was right, she went in for the kill. "Dr. Rice, no doubt you are aware of the litany of crimes against humanity and war crimes that were committed as a direct result of George Bush's decisions and orders. In finality, the judgment of this tribunal will not be based solely on Mr. Bush's causing the war to happen, but also on whether or not acts committed as a result of his war were illegal and thus criminal. We thank you for your testimony and your honesty, Dr. Rice."

With apparent satisfaction for a job well done, Shadid turned toward the bench and stated, "No further questions, Your Honors."

"Thank you, Ms. Shadid," Judge Hurst-Brown said. "Does defense counsel wish to redirect questions to this witness?"

"No, Your Honor, we do not," Ed White responded.

"And do you wish to call any other witnesses?"

"No, sir, we do not."

Hurst-Brown rapped his gavel. "The Prosecutor v. George W. Bush is adjourned until further notice."

8

Family Matters

"Whenever men take the law into their
own hands, the loser is the law. And when
the law loses, freedom languishes."
—ROBERT F. KENNEDY

AMERICA HAS CERTAINLY HAD ITS SHARE of contentious times during its relatively young life: the Civil War of the 1860s, the McCarthy hearings of the 1950s, the Vietnam War of the 1960s and '70s, Democrats versus Republicans, militant blacks versus white racists, male chauvinists versus women's libbers, gays versus straights, and the list goes on. But one of the defining characteristics of Americans is that they permit dissent. Perhaps more than in any other country in the world, diverse citizens are free to express their opinions and advocate for what they believe. America's Founding Fathers fought hard for this right, and many have died for it. It has been a defining characteristic of America's DNA from the start.

This fundamental right was put to the test yet again when a former president of the United States was brought before an international tribunal to stand trial for crimes he may or may not have committed. The story of the Bush trial consumed the public's attention on a level seldom seen in the country's history. It was conversation topic number one at most social gatherings, business meetings, cocktail parties, and political events, before and after church, golf, and bridge games, and PTA, FTA, and AA meetings, you name it. One could not watch, hear, or read media in any form at any time of the day or night without being bombarded with news of the trial. During working hours, people went online, listened to radios, checked mobile devices, sneaked a peek at TV, and discussed and debated developments with anyone willing. The huge monitor in New York City's Times Square provided nonstop real-time coverage of the feed provided by the ICC.

Often it has been observed that humanity has learned its greatest lessons from its most challenging times. One of the enduring and endearing qualities of fair-minded people is that, if presented with the facts and given the opportunity, they can judge right from wrong—and when necessary, alter their opinions in the interest of the common good.

While the case against George W. Bush was yet to be decided, at a minimum it sent a message that heads of governments, large and small, could no longer fight wars without having to face the considered opinion of legal-minded citizens around the world.

At the ICC, it is customary for both the prosecution and defense teams to meet separately during the course of a trial. Much discussion was needed, including an analysis of what had transpired and a debate about the best attack going forward. Late in the evening of an already very long day, the defense team assembled inside the ICC defense conference room. Ed White spoke as he entered.

"Just got off the phone with Don Rumsfeld. He's not coming."

Jonathan Ortloff looked up from a note he was writing.

"What?" Jonathan said. "George W. Bush's secretary of defense refuses to come to the defense of his commander in chief. Bullshit."

Ed shrugged. "He said Condoleezza did a great job, and that Tommy Franks and George know everything he knows. 'Known knowns,' he said, and didn't want to be redundant."

Meredith Lott shook her head. "The truth is he doesn't want to come to The Hague because he could get arrested and put on trial for his advocacy of that war."

"Same could be said for Condoleezza Rice," Jonathan noted, "but she had the guts to come."

As arch as the comments were, they were also true. Just as Bush had been abducted and brought to the ICC to stand trial for his role in the Iraq War, the same fate could await both Rice and Rumsfeld should they venture outside the United States, and in particular, to The Hague.

"Good point," Ed agreed. "Put your finger too close to the fire and you get burned."

Meredith nodded. "Well, we probably saved ourselves a whole bunch of 'known, knowns' and 'unknown, unknowns' and other such gobbledygook."

"Okay, Ms. Lott, what's your take on the status of the case so far?"

"The prosecution is strong, but they stray off base when they focus on *why* George fought the war and not *that* he fought it. The crimes are on trial here, not the reasons for the crimes. I think we should let them go on their merry way, and give them enough rope to hang themselves."

"Agreed," Jonathan said. "I also think McBride is too strident. The judges clearly don't like his attitude, nor do they appreciate him badgering the witnesses. He lets his personal passions get the better of him. Never a good thing in a court of law."

Meredith agreed. "No kidding. He's a loose cannon."

The room was quiet for a moment before Ed asked the question everyone was thinking.

"So, it has to be asked: Should we advise George to testify in his own defense?"

"I say no," Jonathan shot back. "From day one, George's entire posture has been to dismiss the Court's credibility. Putting him on the stand will only undermine that position, and possibly even legitimize the proceedings."

"That may be true," Meredith added, "but we have to remember he's fighting for his freedom, maybe for his life, if he's found guilty and his sentence is long enough. Fighting for what he believes in is what the world has come to expect from George W. Bush, and certainly what Americans expect of him. The strength he showed as a decisive leader on 9/11 in New York City is exactly what we need him to project here and now. For George to sit there and do nothing, say nothing, would tarnish his image, not to mention his legacy."

Ed nodded. "I think you're right. It's just not his style to sit back passively, no matter the odds or how severe the consequences."

"But what about 'command responsibility'?" Jonathan countered. "The prosecution will try to tie George as commander in chief to all potential war crimes committed during the Iraq War."

"We'll have to counter that," Meredith challenged. "Even though he was president and commander in chief, he was several organizational layers above those who were actually making the decisions on the ground that led to those atrocities."

Ed started to pace. "Yes, George will have to make the point continually and forcefully that he did what he did to protect and defend the security of the American people, and for the betterment of the Iraqi society, maybe even the security of the entire Middle East."

Jonathan became more animated. "But won't that just open the door for McBride and Shadid to implicate the neoconservative thinking of Cheney, Rumsfeld, Wolfowitz, and others who may have conspired with George to wage war in the first place?"

"Maybe so," Meredith said, "but if it did, it would confuse and complicate their case and ultimately damage their chances of winning."

They all were noodling the question until Ed looked from Jonathan to Meredith and asked, "Okay, people, guts-ball here. We have to decide: Do we ask George to testify?"

"I say yes," Meredith quickly responded. "I think he would be a forceful voice in his own defense, maybe even critical."

"Jonathan?"

"I still say no. It's a risk we don't have to take—too many traps. They can't get to George unless we put him on the stand."

"But not putting him on the stand could be the very thing that loses the case for us," Ed countered. "George W. Bush is who he is. If he's going down, he's not going down without a fight. I need to discuss this with George and Laura. It's their lives that are at stake."

At the same time the defense team was meeting, the prosecuting attorneys were strolling along a sidewalk in a light drizzle. The lights of the city seen through the gauze of drizzle gave each scene a vague impressionistic quality. Eventually, Nadia asked Michael the question she'd been considering for some time.

"So, you think we're winning?"

"I always think we're winning."

"So sure of yourself?"

"Comes from my mother, for better or worse."

"How so?"

"Every night, when I was a young boy, my mother tucked me into bed and told me how special I was. Mothers . . . you know."

"Not all mothers, unfortunately."

They walked a few more steps in silence.

"What do you worry about?" Nadia asked.

"That it's not what you or I think or say that matters. It's the majority judgment of one man from Great Britain, one woman from Japan, and one man from Nigeria. We can advocate all we want, but all that matters in the end is what they think."

"Seems like Bush can't help his own case if he doesn't testify."

"Yeah, well, he doesn't have to."

"I think he's dead in the water if he doesn't."

"I think he's dead in the water if he *does*."

"Really? You think that?"

Michael stopped and turned to Nadia for emphasis.

"If Bush swears to tell the truth, which he'll have to, the truth will bury him."

"So, you want him to testify?"

"Yes, and we will nail him to the wall."

They stood in the drizzle, studying each other at close range, before Michael added, "If leaders of superpowers get away with waging unnecessary wars with impunity—then humankind is doomed to have more such wars in the future. Simple."

"And fatalistic."

"Guilty as charged."

Later that night, as the drizzle turned into heavy rain, George and Laura Bush sat alone in a Detention Centre meeting room.

"How do you feel about the witness testimonies so far?" Laura asked.

George shrugged. "Okay, I guess. In all wars there's always a lot of collateral damage; easy to find people who were damaged."

"We need to focus on the many people who benefited from the war. No one is talking much about the fact that Iraq is now a democracy."

"This is not so much about humanity or politics as it is about the strict application of international laws."

"Did you ever think you'd be held accountable to those laws?" Laura finally asked.

There was silence in the room for a noticeably long moment before George answered.

"No, I didn't. Neither did other presidents before me."

"George, Ed left a message about wanting to discuss the possibility of you testifying."

"I've been thinking about it."

"Nobody knows more about what you did and why you did it than you. George, you're not a criminal and you're not a murderer. It's just not who you are."

"Here's what I do know: If I don't testify and I am found guilty, it would be horrible, really horrible, for all of us. I could never live with myself if I didn't at least try to defend myself."

"You're a pretty convincing guy when you put your mind to it."

"I couldn't bear the thought of having you, our daughters, our extended families, and the American people suffer the shame of me being found guilty."

"So let's fight it."

Thirty minutes later, Laura Bush sat in a desk chair in her hotel suite engaged in one of the most important conversations of her life. Ed White was pacing.

"Both George and you need to understand that this could be the make-or-break decision of the entire trial," White said.

"We understand, but in our heart of hearts we think it is the right thing to do," Laura replied.

"So, he's willing to testify?"

"Yes. He was already considering it. He's willing to testify, Ed, if you agree it's the right thing to do."

"Honestly, Laura, my team is conflicted. Meredith favors it. Jonathan is opposed."

Studying White carefully, Laura asked, "And you, Ed, what do you think?"

This was the very question Ed White had wrestled with since he first heard about his friend's abduction. In the mix and balance of legal discourse, there was no right or wrong answer, as it would depend on many unknowable variables, most especially what was going on in the minds of the judges. The matter was always going to be a game-day decision, and that day had arrived.

Ed took Laura's hand.

"I have these two thoughts: If in his heart of hearts and in yours it is the right thing to do, then it is the right thing to do. And if it is the right thing to do, then he should do it, and you and George and all the rest of us who love him should never look back. Frankly, if our plan is to do everything we can to win, then he should testify in his own defense. Period. End of statement."

9

In Search of the Truth

"War against a foreign country only happens when the moneyed classes think they are going to profit from it."
—George Orwell

Following the decision that George W. Bush would testify, his defense attorneys requested a one-week recess in order to prepare him for testimony. Consistent with customary legal protocol, the ICC judges granted the request. Concurrently the prosecutors were informed of this, and it set in motion a flurry of preparation by both teams of attorneys.

The world's press, thirsty for blood as always, was not thrilled with the delay and spent the next week in hot debate about the wisdom of Bush's decision. Finally, the most important day of what was now being labeled "the trial of the century" had arrived. Tens of thousands of people from all over the world assembled outside the ICC building in The Hague, either to root for George Bush's innocence or to clamor for his guilt. Inside, the courtroom was jam-packed; the public gallery was standing room only. Laura Bush was escorted into the gallery and discreetly led to an aisle seat in the back row. Presiding Judge Harrison Hurst-Brown announced and gaveled the case back in session, and then invited the defense to call its next witness.

Ed White stood and pronounced with all due gravity, "Thank

you, Your Honor. The defense wishes to call to the witness stand the 43rd president of the United States, Mr. George W. Bush."

As he approached the witness stand, the defendant displayed the supreme confidence of Muhammad Ali entering a boxing ring before a heavyweight championship fight he knew he would win. Bush sat and looked directly at the three ICC judges who would determine his fate. Judge Hurst-Brown asked him to raise his right hand and read the swearing-in document, which he did in a clear and confident voice.

"I, George W. Bush, solemnly declare that I will speak the truth, the whole truth, and nothing but the truth," Bush said.

"Thank you, Mr. Bush. Defense may commence with its questioning."

Bush's longtime friend from Texas, Ed White, smiled at him warmly, nodded at him as if to say, "We got this," and began.

"Mr. President, thank you for your willingness to testify in your defense."

"Very much my pleasure."

White started methodically. "Following the Gulf War in Kuwait that your father, President George H. W. Bush, waged so effectively, UN Resolution 687 required Saddam Hussein to destroy his military arsenal. Can you inform us of what he actually did?"

"Sure. Resolution 687 banned Iraq from possessing biological, chemical, or nuclear weapons or the means to produce them. To ensure compliance, Saddam was required to submit to UN monitoring and verification. At first, Saddam claimed he had only a limited stockpile of chemical weapons and Scud missiles. Over time, UN inspectors discovered a vast arsenal of weapons. Saddam had filled thousands of bombs and warheads with chemical agents. He had a weapons program that was about one year away from producing a nuclear bomb."

White pressed on. "The prosecution has spent a lot of time focusing on the reasons why the Iraq War should not have been fought. Can you tell us the reasons why it was fought?"

"We believed Saddam's weakness was that he loved power and would do anything to keep it. If we could convince him we were serious about removing his regime, there was a chance he would stop producing WMD, end his advocacy of terror, stop harassing his neighbors, and, over time, respect the fundamental human rights of all people. The odds of success were long, but given the alternative, it was worth the effort."

"And can you share with us your strategy?"

"Sure. First, I wanted to rally a coalition of nations to make clear that Saddam's defiance of international obligations was unacceptable. Then, I wanted to develop a credible military option that could be used if he failed to comply. These tracks would run parallel at first, but if the military option became necessary, the tracks would converge. That would be the moment of decision, and ultimately it would be Saddam's to make."

"The 9/11 attacks obviously had a huge effect on all of us. Explain why 9/11 caused you to focus specifically on Saddam Hussein."

"Before 9/11, Saddam was a problem we might have been able to manage. But post-9/11, my view changed. I had just witnessed the damage inflicted by nineteen fanatics, armed with nothing more than box cutters. I could only imagine the destruction possible if an enemy dictator gave his WMD to terrorists. The stakes were too high to trust a ruthless dictator against the current evidence available and the consensus of the world. The lesson of 9/11 was that if we were to wait for a danger to fully materialize, we would be waiting too long."

Observing that his friend was more than up to the task, Ed White amped up the intensity.

"You repeatedly targeted Saddam Hussein as an enemy of the United States and other friendly countries in the world. Other than your own personal feelings, what evidence did you have that led you to focus on him specifically?"

"He was a sworn enemy of the United States. He'd fired at our aircraft, praised 9/11, and tried to assassinate my father. Saddam didn't just violate trivial international demands; he defied sixteen UN resolutions dating back to the nineties. He didn't just rule brutally; he and his henchmen tortured innocent people, raped female political opponents in front of their families, scalded dissidents with acid, and dumped tens of thousands of Iraqis into mass graves. And if all that wasn't enough, he decreed that people who criticized him would have their tongues cut out."

Ed White kept pouring on the coals.

"During the buildup to the Iraq War," White said, "and certainly in these proceedings thus far, much has been said about weapons of mass destruction. Would you please set the record straight about Saddam Hussein's possession of WMD, and perhaps other biological and chemical weapons as well?"

"Absolutely. Saddam didn't just have WMD; he used them. He deployed mustard gas and nerve agents against the Iranians, and massacred more than five thousand innocent Iraqi people in a chemical attack on the Kurdish village of Halabja. The problem was nobody knew what Saddam had done with his biological and chemical stockpiles, especially after he had booted the weapons inspectors out of his country. After reviewing the information available at the time, many intelligence agencies around the world came to the same conclusion we did: Saddam had WMD, and the capacity to produce more."

"And you were in constant communication with your secretary of state, Colin Powell?"

"Yes. Neither of us wanted war. I told Colin that while I was hopeful diplomacy would work, it was possible we would reach a point where war was the only option we had. I asked if he would support military action as a last resort. He said, 'If this is what you have to do, I'm with you, Mr. President.'"

Methodically scoring point after point, White continued.

"You were also in close communication with Prime Minister Tony Blair. You and he agreed to seek a UN resolution to demonstrate support and solidarity from the rest of the world regarding your concerns about Saddam and Iraq."

George Bush seemed to relish the chance to tell his story to both the Court and the worldwide audience he knew would be watching.

"Correct. We told the UN delegation that the world was facing a test, and that the United Nations was at a crucial and defining moment. I posed the question: Are UN Security Council resolutions to be honored and enforced, or to be cast aside without consequence? Will the UN serve its purpose or will it be rendered irrelevant? We needed nine of the fifteen Security Council members without a veto from France, Russia, or China. The vote was unanimous, fifteen to zero, including the United Kingdom, France, Russia, China, and Syria. The world was on record: Saddam had a final opportunity to comply with his obligation to disclose and disarm."

"And if he didn't?"

"He would face serious consequences. Under UN Security Council Resolution 1441, Iraq had thirty days to submit a complete, current, and accurate declaration of all WMD-related programs. The resolution made clear that the burden of proof rested with Saddam. The inspectors did not have to prove that he had weapons. He had to prove that he did not."

"But Saddam never did provide conclusive evidence that he was in compliance with the UN's demand for transparency."

"No, sir, he did not. When he submitted his report, Hans Blix, who led the UN inspections, called it 'rich in volume but poor in information.' Saddam was continuing his pattern of deception. The only way to keep the pressure on him would be for us to present evidence. I asked CIA Director Tenet to brief me on what intelligence we could declassify that would prove Saddam had WMD. Tenet assured me we had sufficient evidence, saying, 'It's a slam dunk.' That's what he said; 'a slam dunk,' and I believed him. I'd been receiving intelligence briefings on Iraq for years. The conclusion that Saddam possessed WMD had universal consensus. My predecessor, Bill Clinton, believed it. Republicans and Democrats on Capitol Hill believed it. Intelligence agencies in Germany, France, the UK, Russia, China, and Egypt believed it."

"And as Saddam showed no interest in complying with UN demands, it made it more apparent than ever that he had something to hide," White added.

Sensing the momentum growing in his favor, Bush turned on his well-known charm.

"Exactly. It became increasingly clear that my prayer for peace would not be answered. Saddam appeared not to have come to a genuine acceptance of the disarmament that was demanded of him. In retrospect, of course, we all should've pushed harder on the intelligence and revisited our assumptions a little more. But at the same time, the evidence and logic pointed in the other direction. I asked myself, if Saddam didn't have WMD, why on Earth would he subject himself to a war he would almost certainly lose?"

"As president of the United States, did you feel you had both the moral authority and the legal authority to wage the Iraq War?"

"Yes, sir, I did, and still do. The US Constitution vests the president with executive power. That power reaches its zenith when wielded to protect national security. Both the United States Congress and the United Nations provided the legal authority and the moral authority necessary to wage the war. No debate about that."

White let those words hang in the room for a moment before continuing.

"Mr. Bush, you've been accused of war crimes. But in truth you were only trying to protect and defend the citizens of the United States, which you were elected to do."

"I was trying in the best way I knew how. The fundamental questions I know people ask are whether or not we won that war, whether or not democracy won, and will it take hold in Iraq? And will it change people's attitudes in the future? I believe it will. History has proven that democracies can change societies. The classic case I like to cite is Japan. Prime Minister Koizumi is one of my best friends. I find it interesting that he joined me as a peacemaker on a variety of issues, and yet my father fought the Japanese in World War II, when Japan was a sworn enemy of the United States. Today, Japan is an ally of peace, a Japanese-style democracy."

"Thank you, Mr. President." White turned confidently to the ICC judges and said, "No further questions at this time, Your Honors."

"Thank you, Mr. White," Hurst-Brown announced. "The prosecution may proceed with its cross-examination."

McBride and Shadid exchanged supportive nods. McBride stood and addressed the judges.

"Thank you, Your Honors."

And just like that, after more than a year of research, study, investigation, preparation, and planning, the moment for George W. Bush to be held accountable for the war crimes of which he was accused had arrived. McBride turned to Bush and began.

"Mr. Bush, I know you're a big sportsman and love to play games. So I'm going to set out the rules of this game, in case you don't know them. All crimes in international law require two elements. The first is criminal intent, referred to as *mens rea*. Criminal intent must include specific elements such as malice aforethought, intention, and knowing. The second is the prohibited act, referred to as *actus reus*. The prohibited acts in your case include willful killing, imprisonment, persecution, causing great bodily injury and suffering, extensive destruction of property not justified by military necessity, depriving prisoners of a fair trial, and torture, especially of prisoners, and the other specified crimes that have been provided to you and your defense counsel.

"While all these crimes are deplorable, I note in particular your culpability in connection with Iraqi prisoner abuse at the Abu Ghraib prison. Any person who knows the truth will know that the inhumane and illegal prisoner abuse used by American soldiers in your war caused more damage to America's reputation around the world than any other single event in its history.

"So the questions to be answered, Mr. Bush, in order to establish your guilt would be: First, did you as president of the United States and commander in chief of all military operations personally and directly cause the Iraq War to happen? Second, what were the circumstances of your war that led to the inevitable killing of human beings? And, third, what were the consequences of your war in terms of human death, property damaged or destroyed, and, last but not least, prisoner abuses."

McBride turned to the judges and looked each in the eye for

a few seconds, no doubt to emphasize the universal and historical significance of the testimony about to be given.

"Your Honors, no one was publically advocating war with Iraq until the defendant George W. Bush started talking about it. It all started with George W. Bush creating something out of nothing. The prosecution will prove that George W. Bush caused the Iraq War, and that under international law he must bear the responsibility for the deaths and collateral damage to nonmilitary property resulting from that war.

"We understand that waging war is not necessarily a crime in and of itself, but the human deaths and physical destruction due to war are indeed included in the definitions of crimes against humanity and war crimes. For those who do not know and are interested, the complete definition of war crimes is set forth in the Rome Statute of the International Criminal Court. Article 7 states that crimes against humanity are acts committed as part of a widespread or systematic attack against a civilian population, including murder, extermination, enslavement, torture, rape, and the list goes on. Article 8 defines war crimes as willful killing, torture, or inhuman treatment causing great suffering or serious injury, extensive destruction and appropriation of property not justified by military necessity, intentionally directing attacks on the civilian population, and the list goes on.

"The basic premise of this case is this: George W. Bush's armed conflict with Iraq lasted eight years and nine months, during which approximately forty-five hundred American soldiers, hundreds of Iraqi and coalition soldiers, and hundreds of thousands of Iraqi citizens—with some estimates reaching well beyond a million Iraqi citizens—were murdered. All of this is to say that if it can be proven that the defendant, George W. Bush, was the single person most responsible for causing the war to happen, and that crimes against humanity or war crimes were in fact committed, then he is criminally liable for those crimes."

McBride turned to address the entire courtroom.

"George Bush's initial justification for going to war was that Saddam Hussein had WMD. After it became incontrovertibly evident during the lead-up to the war that Iraq did not have WMD, Mr. Bush shifted his reasoning to the notion that Saddam Hussein was an imminent threat to the security of the United States. When that was proven to be absent of any physical evidence and totally unlikely, he shifted his story yet again to the higher moral ground of trying to save Iraqi citizens from their leader, Saddam Hussein, specifically referring to regime change."

Finally, McBride turned back to the defendant and began his questioning.

"So, George W. Bush, to get you on the record at last, why did you take America to war with Iraq?"

Bush responded immediately and forcefully.

"Following the attacks of 9/11, I made an important decision: The United States would consider any nation that harbored terrorists to be responsible for the acts of those terrorists. Specifically regarding Iraq, my position was that we should be optimistic that diplomacy and international pressure would succeed in disarming Saddam Hussein's regime. But we couldn't allow him to have weapons of mass destruction. I would not let that happen."

"Will you concede once and for all that Saddam Hussein did not have WMD in 2003, the year you started your war?"

"It's easy for you to arrogantly state now that he didn't have WMD. But if you were charged with protecting two hundred and ninety million Americans, and you weren't sure he didn't have them, and that the last time you'd checked he did have them, you wouldn't be so cocksure of yourself."

"Mr. Bush, on September 20, 2001, nine days after 9/11, you said in a congressional address, 'Americans are asking, "Who attacked our country?" The evidence all points to a collection of loosely affiliated terrorist organizations known as al Qaeda.' That's what you said. So you knew it was al Qaeda that was responsible for the 9/11 attacks, and Saddam Hussein had nothing to do with it?"

"We believed Saddam might have been in cahoots with al Qaeda."

"But in that speech to Congress you didn't mention Saddam even once. Why not? You mentioned only al Qaeda, which, as everybody knew even then, was founded and led by Osama bin Laden."

"We went after al Qaeda. Most of them were in Afghanistan. Less than a month after 9/11, in October 2001, we started a war in Afghanistan. Our goals were to remove the Taliban and destroy al Qaeda."

"According to your secretary of state, most of the ground fighting was outsourced to Afghan warlords and security forces. Why didn't you use the full force of the United States military to bring the 9/11 perpetrators to justice?"

"We used the military strategy we thought best for the task, especially given the physical challenges in Afghanistan and the nature of the enemy."

"After trying unsuccessfully to get Osama bin Laden, you eventually dismissed him. But in order to kill a snake, don't you have to take out its head?"

"I didn't know if bin Laden was hiding in some cave somewhere or not. Deep in my heart I knew the man was on the run, if he was even alive at all."

"But you didn't destroy al Qaeda, and you didn't take out bin Laden. So in that respect, you failed in your obligation to the

American people to seek out and destroy the very people who committed the atrocities of 9/11. When bin Laden was spotted in the Tora Bora region, why didn't you take him out then?"

"Because terror is about more than one person," Mr. Bush answered, growing increasingly impatient. "The idea of focusing on one person indicates to me that people don't understand the scope of the mission."

"In an interview in the Oval Office, in December 2001, three months after 9/11, you said we're going to 'get Osama bin Laden dead or alive. Either way, it doesn't matter to me.' If you had done just that, we wouldn't be here today. Instead you turned to Saddam Hussein, who had never directly terrorized America or Americans."

"Obviously, I judged Saddam, given his past record, to be a bigger problem at the time."

"Mr. Bush, respectfully, that doesn't make any sense. There was no evidence that Saddam had WMD since the 1990s. If you were going to ignore al Qaeda and bin Laden and target another regime that was a problem, why not Bashar al-Assad in Syria, or Kim Jong Il in North Korea? It would've made about the same amount of sense as targeting Saddam Hussein. Was it because you realized that bin Laden and al Qaeda would be a long, complicated fight, so you targeted Saddam instead because he was old and weak by then and you wanted to prove yourself a strong, decisive president, boldly responding to 9/11?"

"That is a ridiculous allegation. After 9/11, I had to send a clear message to other terrorist organizations around the world that they couldn't attack America and get away with it. They had to pay the price. You obviously don't understand the geopolitical realities of the time."

"One of us doesn't, that's for sure," McBride snapped back.

The exchange had gotten personal. The air crackled with the

intensity, and everyone watching inside and out of the courtroom was riveted. McBride continued his assault.

"The truth is you took America's thirst for revenge after 9/11, pivoted attention away from bin Laden, and directed it toward Saddam. The initial reason you gave for invading Iraq was that Saddam had WMD and posed an imminent threat to the security of the United States. Mr. Bush, this brings us to a critically important issue in this proceeding: What you knew, and when you knew it. I call your attention to the declassified Joint Chiefs of Staff INR intelligence report entitled 'Iraq: Status of WMD Programs' that was prepared and circulated in September 2002, six months before you ordered the invasion of Iraq. Under oath and in plain view of all peace-loving people of the world, George W. Bush, did you receive that report?"

"As president, I received many intelligence reports from many sources."

"Were you apprised of the details contained in that Joint Chiefs' report?"

"I just said I got many reports. I couldn't possibly remember the specific details of each."

"Did you read or were you made aware of the following intel regarding Iraq's military capabilities that were contained in that report: 'Our knowledge of the Iraqi weapons program is based largely, perhaps 90 percent, on analysis of imprecise intelligence'?"

Breaking protocol, defense attorney White interrupted the proceedings to offer legal advice to his friend. "George, you don't have to answer these questions," he said.

Judge Hurst-Brown responded immediately. "Mr. White, you will be held in contempt if that sort of thing happens again. Prosecution may continue."

Undeterred, McBride ratcheted up the pressure.

"More from the Joint Chief's report: 'Our assessments rely heavily on analytic assumptions and judgment rather than hard evidence. We do not know with confidence the location of any nuclear-weapon-related facilities. We cannot confirm the identity of any Iraqi facilities that produce, test, fill, or store biological weapons.' Furthermore, both UN and US weapons inspectors scouring Iraq before the war came to the same conclusion: Saddam did not posses WMD, having disposed of them after the Gulf War in 1991. The question is, George Bush, when you alleged that Saddam had WMD, were you cherry-picking the facts or were you outright lying?"

"Objection, Your Honors!" White interrupted. "Badgering the witness."

Bush answered before the judges could speak.

"There were as many intelligence experts that thought Saddam had WMD as not. I was not going to play Russian roulette with the lives of the American people."

"Tragically, the allegation that Saddam had WMD became the basis of the misleading propaganda you started force-feeding Congress and the American people—the facts, according to George W. Bush."

"People have different recollections of history. It depended on which intelligence sources you believed and what your point of view was."

"Nonsense. The truth is the truth. If no one could prove he had WMD, and he hadn't had them for more than a decade, then he didn't have them!"

Bush offered no comment. The two equally intent and forceful combatants just glared at each other.

"After your allegations that Saddam had WMD were proven

false," McBride continued, "and everybody knew Saddam was not then and had never been a direct threat to the security of the United States, you changed your tune and started to advocate that coalition forces should free the Iraqi people and thus allow free elections, which would lead to democracy in Iraq."

"Our belief was that if Iraq could become a democracy, other countries in the region might follow."

"So even though the majority of Muslim-based Middle Eastern countries had not embraced democracy for thousands of years, George W. Bush early in the twenty-first century, after having ravaged the country of Iraq with eight and a half years of war, was hoping it would magically embrace democracy?"

Bush looked insulted by such a condescending assertion from McBride and punched back. "Germany embraced democracy after World War II," Bush said.

"Germany was not a Muslim country," McBride counter-punched. "And the Allied powers basically made democracy a condition of surrender. If you had said when you first started your drumbeat for war that it was to provide Iraqis with free elections, you knew Americans would never have bought that as a justification for invading Iraq. Americans are not stupid. If that was reason enough for going to war, during the past fifty years America would have been fighting wars all over the world: China, Iran, North Korea, Cambodia, Darfur, Myanmar, Cuba, just to name a few. The fact is that the majority of member states in the United Nations disapproved of your war."

"Many world leaders shared my assessment of the threat Iraq posed: Tony Blair of the UK, John Howard of Australia, José María Aznar of Spain, Junichiro Koizumi of Japan, Jan Peter Balkenende of the Netherlands, Anders Fogh Rasmussen of Denmark, and most other leaders in Central and Eastern Europe."

McBride countered. "However, France, Germany, Russia, China, and the majority of member nations in the UN refused to go along with your obsession to wage that war."

"France had significant economic interest in Iraq. I was not surprised when President Chirac cautioned against using military force against Iraq. If Saddam Hussein had one friend in the world, it was Jacques Chirac. If you checked the facts, Mr. McBride, you would see that Iraq purchased something like twenty-five billion dollars' worth of military equipment from France. The problem with Chirac's logic was that without the credible threat of force, diplomacy would be toothless and Saddam Hussein would escape the scrutiny of the free world once again."

"But the reality is that France never opposed war with Iraq; it only opposed your mad rush to war. President Chirac knew it would enrage Arabic and Islamic public opinion and, as he said, 'create a large number of little bin Ladens.' In a joint interview with CBS and CNN on March 16, 2003, four days before you invaded Iraq, Mr. Chirac said, 'We feel there is another option, another more normal way, a less dramatic way than war. And we should pursue it until we have come to a dead end.' Russia opposed your war as well?"

"Putin didn't consider Saddam a threat and didn't want to jeopardize Russia's lucrative oil contracts with Iraq."

"German Chancellor Gerhard Schröder denounced the use of force against Iraq. His justice minister said, 'Bush wants to divert attention from domestic political problems. Hitler also did that.'"

"That was bullshit. Hard to think of anything more insulting than being compared to Hitler by a German official."

McBride picked up a binder of documents he would refer to frequently.

"In your first State of the Union address, on January 29, 2002, you spoke of preventing, and I quote, 'regimes that sponsor terror from threatening America or her friends with weapons of mass destruction.' You mentioned North Korea and Iran, and then said, 'Iraq continues to flaunt its hostility toward America and to support terror. States like these constitute an axis of evil arming to threaten the peace of the world.' So, just four months after 9/11, when Americans wanted justice for the terrorists responsible for the attack, you started targeting North Korea, Iran, and Iraq. Why?"

"Because I was focused on the regimes I thought represented the greatest threat to America and her allies at the time."

"For the record, Mr. Bush, not one of the countries in your 'axis of evil' has lifted a finger to harm America or endanger the peace of the world years after you threatened they would. But back to the question, which I am going to keep asking until we get a coherent answer, four months after the 9/11 attacks, which Iraq had nothing to do with, why did you switch the country's attention from al Qaeda and bin Laden to Saddam Hussein?"

"Saddam had plotted to develop anthrax, nerve gas, and nuclear weapons for over a decade. He had used poison gas to murder thousands of his own citizens. His was a regime that agreed to international inspections and then kicked out the inspectors. This was a regime that had something to hide from the rest of the world."

"But it has been proven repeatedly that Saddam didn't have anything to hide. Inspectors were given access to every site they asked to visit. Hans Blix said, and I quote, 'On no particular occasion were we denied access.' In total, UN and US inspectors conducted more that nine hundred inspections at over five hundred sites and found nothing."

No response from Bush.

"In addition to allowing unfettered inspections," McBride continued, "Saddam had done nothing to harm or threaten the United

States or its allies since the 1990s, more than a decade before the time in question. In your second State of the Union address, on January 29, 2003, one and a half months before your war, you referred to 9/11 as follows: 'In the ruins of two towers, at the western wall of the Pentagon, and on a field in Pennsylvania, this nation made a pledge, and we renew that pledge tonight: Whatever the duration of this struggle and whatever the difficulties, we will not permit the triumph of violence in the affairs of men.' Then you again pivoted away from bin Laden and al Qaeda, saying, 'We have called on the United Nations to fulfill its charter and stand by its demand that Iraq disarm.' Iraq? In that speech, you didn't mention Osama bin Laden or al Qaeda even once, but incredibly you did mention Iraq five times and Saddam Hussein thirty-one times. How could that be?"

"There was some ambiguity in the international community about Hussein, and I wanted to clear it up. Either he would come clean about his WMD or there would be war."

"You then moved this bait and switch of yours to the international stage with desperate scaremongering and dire warnings. In a speech you gave to the UN General Assembly on September 12, 2002, you described Iraq as 'a grave and gathering danger.' Then, again, falsely creating the impression that Iraq had something to do with 9/11, you said, 'The attacks of September 11 would be a prelude to far greater horrors.' Again the question: Why Saddam Hussein, and not al Qaeda and bin Laden?"

"I told you," Bush said, clearly running out of patience. "I didn't know where bin Laden was. We were going after al Qaeda at large. I was truly not concerned about bin Laden. I knew he was on the run. But once we set out our policy and started executing the plan, we shoved him more and more to the margins."

"And eventually turned your total focus to war with Iraq?"

"Yes, because, as I said, that's where I determined the greatest threat to be. Leaders must utilize estimates and opinions of top military advisors to make the tough decisions necessary to protect their countries. There is hardly ever a decision that is 100 percent right or 100 percent wrong. You're always dealing with percentages of the optimum, seeking to find the best possible outcome in the situation you're confronted with."

Bush sat back with a smug expression, presumably because he had calculated that, while he may not have won this critically important exchange, he hadn't lost it either. McBride, evidencing both frustration and anger, pressed on.

"Mr. Bush, without an acceptable answer to this central question, we're going to leave this issue to the judgment of the three judges, and perhaps the people around the world who are following this case, and maybe even historians who will look back upon this case in the future."

McBride shuffled through some papers and started a new offensive.

"Let me ask you this: Why the incredible rush to your war? The UN inspectors were making good progress and Saddam was giving them unlimited access. Why the rush? Surely you didn't think Saddam would launch a nuclear attack on the United States while UN and US inspectors were swarming all over his country. And WMD, if he had any, which he didn't, would have a maximum strike range of ninety miles. Iraq is half the circumference of the world away from the United States. On top of that, one of your top generals, Anthony Zinni, said at the time that containment was, and I quote, 'working remarkably well.'"

"For more than a year," Bush said, "I had tried to address the threat from Saddam Hussein without going to war. We obtained a UN resolution making it clear there would be serious consequences if he continued to defy us. I gave Saddam and his sons forty-eight hours to avoid war. He rejected every opportunity. The only logical conclusion was that he did have something to hide, something so important that he was willing to go to war to conceal it. I knew the consequences my order would bring, but letting a sworn enemy of America refuse to account for his weapons of mass destruction was a risk I could not afford to take."

"Your Honors," McBride said, turning to address the judges, "I'd like to call your attention to the sentence George Bush just said regarding his knowing the consequences his orders would bring, and request the Court reporter read back that exact sentence, starting with 'I knew.'"

Hurst-Brown instructed the court reporter to read the sentence. She backed up her dictation machine to the exact point and began.

"'I knew the consequences my order would bring,'" the court reporter read, "'but letting a sworn enemy of America refuse to account for his weapons of mass destruction was a risk I could not afford to take.'"

"Thank you," McBride said. "Your Honors, the sentence is evidence of George W. Bush's malice aforethought, which is required to prove criminal intent." He turned back to Bush. "You knew Saddam Hussein did not have the military capacity to attack the United States at the time in question. On December 28, 2002, three months before your war, General Franks compared Iraq's state of combat readiness in 1991, the beginning of the Gulf War, to its combat readiness in 2003, the beginning of your war. We'll use this chart for clarity, and note it is submitted as Prosecution Evidence #3."

The ICC judges and all others turned their attention to the video monitors in the courtroom as McBride began to read the chart.

156

"SOLDIERS: 1991—over 1,000,000. 2003—350,000. TANKS: 1991—6,000. 2003—2,600. ROCKET LAUNCHERS AND GUNS: 1991—4,000. 2003—2,700."

McBride continued with renewed resolve.

"Quite aside from the fact that Iraq had reduced capacity in terms of manpower and weaponry, America had grown much stronger. Quoting General Franks, 'Not only is Iraq's military smaller and less well-equipped, but advances in America's precision weapons made our forces much more capable.' All of this meaning, Your Honors, that not only did Iraq have virtually zero capacity to attack the United States, it had very little capacity to defend itself.

"Mr. Bush, the results of your mighty war against the Iraqi people were that the capital city Baghdad fell in three weeks, the iconic statue of Saddam Hussein was pulled to the ground in a month, and Saddam was captured in nine months, which meant the war for all practical purposes, was over. And so, knowing all that, for the love of God, why were you in such a rush? Why didn't you just wait, as many world leaders pleaded for you to do, and let UN inspectors take another few weeks to complete their inspections? Not months, but a few weeks?"

"Three months before the invasion, Tony Blair and I agreed that Saddam had violated the UN Security Council Resolution by submitting a false declaration," Bush said with obvious disdain. "We had ample justification to enforce the 'serious consequences' provision in Resolution 1441. We had experienced the horror of September 11. We had seen that those who hate America were willing to crash airplanes into tall buildings full of innocent people. We couldn't afford to wait."

"You couldn't afford to wait?" McBride said, raising his voice. "Really? Couldn't wait a few weeks, or couldn't control your hysterical obsession to take out Saddam Hussein?"

"Objection, Your Honors," White interjected. "Badgering the witness."

"Objection sustained," Hurst-Brown agreed.

"Mr. Bush," McBride continued, "since you and your closest advisors had never fought in a war—not Dick Cheney, not Don Rumsfeld, and not Condoleezza Rice—and with so many experienced military minds in America pleading for restraint, did you ever stop to consider you could accomplish your goals without having to send America's sons and daughters to fight a massively destructive war?"

McBride had touched a sensitive nerve. Bush shot back in anger.

"This line of questioning is a bunch of crap. I was in constant communication with my Joint Chiefs of Staff. The overwhelming consensus was that we had to engage in the war to obtain our stated objectives."

Sensing Bush was losing his composure, McBride attacked with increased intensity.

"No, the truth is that going to war was not the overwhelming consensus of the US military until you convinced them you were going to war and, out of respect for the presidency and loyalty to duty, they went along with you. They did what you made them do as their commander in chief.

"Besides, there's a difference between the military and the leader of the nation, whose job it is to gain the greatest advantage while sacrificing the least in terms of lives lost, money spent, and damage to civilization. Presidents Eisenhower, Kennedy, Reagan, and Clinton all knew that dealing with adversaries across the negotiating table was a better way to promote America's values and improve security rather than resorting to war. Those presidents understood that fair-minded, tough diplomacy, and economic sanctions were strengths, not weakness, and that exhausting diplomatic options before sending troops into battle was a fundamental responsibility of leadership. The cost of your departure from those basic concepts of human decency reverberates around the world even to this day."

"You have a far too simplistic view of world diplomacy and, frankly, I think a dangerous one. You don't negotiate with proven terrorists like Saddam Hussein."

"You also don't attack the elected president of a sovereign country and remove him just because you don't like him. Mr. Bush, in a televised address you gave on March 17, 2003, three days before your war, you said, 'Intelligence gathered by this and other governments leaves no doubt that the Iraq regime continues to possess and conceal some of the most lethal weapons ever devised.' That was not true, as has been proven. You continued, 'Responding to such enemies only after they have struck is not self-defense; it is suicide. The security of the world requires disarming Saddam Hussein now.'"

Bush seemed to expect this issue and countered aggressively.

"Two months before the invasion, Hans Blix told the United Nations that his inspectors had discovered warheads that Saddam had failed to declare or destroy, and they found indications of the highly toxic VX nerve agent, used to make mustard gas. The Iraqi government was defying the inspections process. It had violated Resolution 1441 by blocking U-2 flights and hiding three thousand documents in the home of an Iraqi nuclear official."

"It is astonishing," McBride opined, "how the intelligence you used was at such variance with most other US government sources and her allies. Can we agree at least that the intel from US and international sources was conflicted?"

"Yes."

"No one could know for sure what Saddam's capacity was at that time?"

"Presidents have to make tough decisions based on the intel they receive. That's what I did as the duly elected president and commander in chief."

"So, your decision to wage war with Iraq was nothing more than a calculated risk based on your interpretation of conflicting intel? Factored into that calculation needed to be the risk of being wrong! Human lives, many of them, were at stake. Sons and daughters of American families would be killed by the thousands. George W. Bush, if your calculation would've included sending your own daughters to war, would you have been so willing to commit American troops?"

Ed White stood. "Objection, Your Honors," he said. "Not relevant."

"Objection sustained," Judge Hurst-Brown agreed.

Bush glared at the prosecutor. "Watch yourself, McBride," he said.

McBride ignored him, stating, "You must've known Saddam had only engaged in regional wars with his neighbors—Iran in the eighties and Kuwait in the nineties. He never invaded other countries or really even threatened to invade other countries. Not Israel. Not Saudi Arabia. And certainly not the United States."

"He invaded Israel. Get your facts right."

"He lobbed a couple of bombs at Israel. He never invaded with ground troops. Virtually every US administration before you had cooperated with repressive governments in the region including Saudi Arabia, Egypt, even Iraq. So, George W. Bush, let's set the record straight once and for all. Did you attack Iraq to protect Israel?"

"No matter how many times you ask questions of that nature, my answer to all of them will be the same."

"To protect your friends and longtime family business associates in Saudi Arabia?"

No response.

"To protect Middle East oil production critical to American businesses?"

Again, no response.

"To gain revenge against Saddam Hussein for attempting to kill your father?"

Finally, Bush responded.

"All of the above, and to protect the American people from the threat of a known terrorist."

"But none of that required or justified a full-on war. If you were so concerned about Saddam Hussein, you could've sent in Special Ops forces and taken him out in a matter of days. Or was it that you knew a war with Iraq would be hugely expensive and thus hugely profitable for America's military-industrial complex?"

Ed White stood to rescue his client. "Objection, Your Honors. Conjecture."

"Overruled," Hurst-Brown answered. "Prosecution may continue."

"For the record, in the first full year of the defendant's war, 2004, American taxpayers spent 542.4 billion dollars on defense. In total, his war cost Americans more than four trillion dollars. That's a 't' as in 'trillion,' not a 'b' as in 'billion.'"

"The cost of freedom is not cheap," Bush countered with noted condescension.

"Corporations that supplied the US military with guns and vehicles and protective armor and food and so on, corporations like Lockheed Martin, Boeing, General Dynamics, Raytheon,

Halliburton, made ungodly amounts of money," McBride said. "Stock prices rose to new heights. Friends of yours who were fat cats got even fatter. The US economy boomed. All good news for your mid-war reelection campaign, which, of course, you won. And all of this insane profiteering done at the cost of precious human lives and America's treasury."

"I resent the implication."

"Resent it all you want, but isn't it true?"

"If you believe in the universality of freedom, as I do, then you believe that those of us who are free have an obligation to free those who are not. Saddam Hussein was a bully and a murderer. You can find plenty of Iraqis who will tell you how thankful they are to be no longer living under his tyranny."

"There are many more Iraqis who would say removing Saddam is one thing, but invading and occupying their country is another thing altogether, and something virtually none of them wanted. Mr. Bush, I'm sure you know that America's 34th president, President Dwight D. Eisenhower, spoke of a deep-seated fear he had after World War II, saying, and I quote, 'In the councils of government we must guard against the acquisition of unwarranted influence, whether sought or unsought, by the military-industrial complex. The potential for the disastrous rise of misplaced power exists and will persist.'"

"Of course. I'm well aware of this speech."

"But you chose to ignore it."

Bush didn't take the bait and glared back in return.

"The American Declaration of Independence states, among other things, that all men are created equal, that they are endowed by their creator with certain unalienable rights, and that among these are life, liberty, and the pursuit of happiness," McBride said. "Do you believe, Mr. Bush, that America's

Founding Fathers intended those rights to be just for Americans, or for all people?"

Defense attorney White stood. "Objection, Your Honors. The prosecution is spouting irrelevant American history that has no bearing on this case."

Hurst-Brown disagreed. "Objection overruled."

"Your Honor," White persisted, "with respect, the defendant has been subjected to sustained questioning for a noticeably long period of time. In the interest of fair treatment of a former president of the United States who is now a defendant in your Court, defense requests a recess."

McBride approached the bench. "Your Honors, prosecution objects and pleads that recess is not granted. We are in the middle of cross-examination, and there is much to cover."

"The Court recognizes the prosecution's objection," Hurst-Brown replied, "but also recognizes it is an appropriate time to recess." He rapped his gavel twice and announced, "Defense request is granted. Court is adjourned until 9:00 AM tomorrow, at which time we will reconvene for further questioning by the prosecution."

Following the abrupt recess, international news organizations scrambled to get their reporters on camera to recap the dramatic developments of the day. As the case had generated a huge amount of interest, the lineup of camera crews representing the world's top broadcasters had grown noticeably.

"Even though George W. Bush and his cabinet waged the Iraq War," China's CCTV correspondent Cheng Lee Teoh commented, "it was pointed out that most of them had no firsthand experience in war combat. Mr. Bush himself, seeking to avoid the Vietnam War, served in the Texas Air National Guard but was suspended for failing to take a physical examination. Vice President Cheney received student deferments during the Vietnam War, allowing him to avoid military service. And National Security Advisor, Condoleezza Rice, pursued her higher education, obtaining a bachelor's degree from the University of Denver, and a master's degree from Notre Dame. It is hard to understand how government officials can effectively lead a military without having any firsthand military experience themselves. Such a thing would never happen in China, where everybody serves."

Iraq's top TV commentator, Omar Kassab, stated, "As we watch the trial in The Hague, it is interesting to note the public's opinion in the United States of George W. Bush's war. Regarding the way he handled the Iraq War, 73 percent of Americans said they disapproved. When Mr. Bush left office, he had the lowest approval rating of any president in history: 22 percent. Noting that the decision in the Bush case requires at least two of three judges to find him guilty, perhaps these polling percentages provide some insight as to how the ICC judges might rule. Perhaps not."

Back at the ICC building, the defense and prosecution teams were using the evening recess to prepare for the following morning. In the defense meeting room, Ed White was reminding his client about optimum courtroom protocol.

"George, you gotta remain consistent with your testimony. McBride will try to catch you in a discrepancy to create the impression that other claims you've made are inaccurate."

Meredith Lott nodded, adding, "You're doing well, George, but just state the facts, sparingly and simply. Don't feel you need to elaborate. It will make the prosecution's job even harder."

Jonathan Ortloff chimed in. "Also, regardless of what McBride says or does, try to avoid attacking him back. Yes, he is an arrogant and pretentious asshole, but if the judges sense hostility from you, it's possible they could make a subliminal deduction that your frustration comes from guilt rather than anger."

"Remember that we follow the prosecution with cross-examination," Meredith said. "We will provide you plenty of opportunity to state your case clearly and completely, and of course, advocate for your innocence."

"Most importantly, we need to remain cognizant that the prosecution bears the burden of proof," Ed reminded his colleagues. "If the evidence is circumstantial or parenthetical, or if the questioning is observed to be accusatory rather than fact-finding, it will hurt their chances of winning."

"I feel like a boxer getting instructions from his corner between rounds of a heavyweight fight," Bush observed.

Ed smiled reassuringly. "Sorry, George. It's just that there's a lot to cover and little time to do it. I would also urge you to start playing to the judges more. Try to establish more person-to-person contact. Look at them more. Maybe even smile once in a while, like everything's going to be okay. After all, your fate will be determined by their collective opinion."

10

Back in the Saddle

"Truth is incontrovertible. Panic may resent it.
Ignorance may deride it. Malice may
distort it. But there it is."

—WINSTON CHURCHILL

AT 9:00 AM SHARP ON THE FOLLOWING MORNING, Judge Harrison Hurst-Brown rapped his gavel and proclaimed, "The Prosecutor v. George W. Bush is back in session. Prosecution questioning of the accused may continue."

"Thank you, Your Honor," Michael McBride replied. He then turned to the defendant and abruptly restarted his questioning.

"Mr. Bush, did you ask your vice president, Dick Cheney, or secretary of defense, Donald Rumsfeld, about the wisdom of going to war?"

"I didn't need to ask their opinion," George Bush shot back. "If you had been sitting where I was sitting, you would have seen pretty clearly what they were thinking."

"Surely you must have asked the most trusted and respected member of your cabinet, the only member of your administration who had fought in a war, Secretary of State Colin Powell?

"I knew where Colin stood. I didn't agree with him."

"The fact is that you were hell-bent on having your war, regardless of what others thought. Isn't that correct, Mr. Bush?"

"That's absurd," Bush replied in anger. "While the world is

undoubtedly safer with Saddam gone, the reality is, I sent troops into combat based on intelligence that proved to be false."

Silence fell over the courtroom. It was the first time George W. Bush had admitted guilt of any kind in connection to the war. McBride remained silent, hoping Bush would say more, and sure enough he did.

"That was a massive blow to our credibility, my credibility, and it shook the confidence of the American people. No one was more shocked or angry than I was when we didn't find WMD. I got a sickening feeling in my stomach every time I thought about it. I still do."

McBride waited a few seconds to let Bush's admission of guilt resonate in the courtroom, and then addressed the only people in the world whose opinions would matter in the determination of his guilt or innocence.

"Your Honors, Mr. Bush just admitted that there never were WMD in Iraq, and thus, the basis he relied upon to wage his war was never true, meaning it was false, meaning his war was illegal, meaning he is guilty of war crimes. For clarity, Your Honors, I ask that the court reporter read back Mr. Bush's testimony, beginning with 'the reality is,' please."

Ed White had to interject, and he did. "Objection, Your Honors, cause for speculation."

"Objection overruled," Hurst-Brown replied, and turned to discuss the matter *sotto voce* with his fellow judges. Two minutes later, Hurst-Brown addressed the Court. "The prosecution's request is granted. Would the court reporter please comply with the prosecution's request?"

"Yes, Your Honor," the court reporter replied and read, "'the reality is, I sent troops into combat based on intelligence that proved to be false.'"

"Thank you, Your Honors," McBride said, and quickly moved on. "As we know, in international criminal law, in order to prove guilt, criminal intent at the time of the crime has to be proven. In law, the word 'intent' means 'the state of a person's mind that directs his or her actions toward a specific objective.' According to the admissions George W. Bush just made, the intelligence he used was wrong, and there were no WMD in Iraq. Let's consider that in connection with 'intent.' If Mr. Bush was intent on a fair and honest assessment of Saddam's present-time capability before committing human lives and his nation's treasury to armed warfare, he would have to be certain the intelligence was accurate, not questionable, not debatable, not conflicted, not disputed, but certain. And even though the intelligence community could not find WMD, George W. Bush, as president of the United States, gave the order to start the Iraq War. Without him, there never would've been a war.

"Your Honors, I would like to direct your attention to an interview the accused did with ABC's Diane Sawyer in December 2003, nine months into his war. Ms. Sawyer asked Mr. Bush to make a distinction between Saddam *having* WMD as opposed to the *possibility* he could acquire them. Mr. Bush said, 'What's the difference? If he were to acquire weapons, he would be the danger.'

"Please note carefully, Mr. Bush said, 'If he were to acquire weapons.' That's what George W. Bush said in a live television interview nine months into his war: *If he were to acquire.* Your Honors, the defendant just admitted that he ordered his war on the mere possibility Saddam had WMD. And if he didn't know with certainty that Saddam had WMD, then his intent was to fight his war regardless of this lack of evidence. He knowingly lied to the American people, the United States Congress, and the UN. The eventual approval of the US Congress was secured as a result of false accusations made by the defendant. And without valid approvals from Congress and the UN, Mr. Bush's presidential order to fight his war was illegal, making his war a criminal act."

Bush punched back. "You can't just take questions and answers and spin 'em out of context any way you want just to try to prove your point."

McBride ignored Bush's comment and continued.

"The domino effect of this man's war is as follows: He removed Saddam from power and in the process upset the balance of power that had existed in the region for years. George Bush's plan for creating a democracy in Iraq was never going to happen because the majority of Iraqis didn't want a democracy. Anger over his unnecessary and illegal war, coupled with his arrogant attempt to influence the beliefs of Islamic people, emboldened al Qaeda and spawned new terrorist groups, such as the Islamic State, also known as ISIS, which basically hates everything about America and Americans. Mr. Bush, what do you think would've happened if you had just taken out bin Laden and destroyed al Qaeda instead of waging war on Iraq? Have you ever stopped to think about how different the world would be if you had just done that?"

Bush didn't respond.

"If you hadn't insisted on waging your war, more than a million people would still be alive today and tens of thousands would not be suffering from the physical or mental wounds caused by your war. And most probably, an uneasy peace would still exist in the region."

"What would've happened if Iraq had fallen to al Qaeda? You ever think about that?" Bush finally replied.

"That's an absurd question," McBride countered. "After al Qaeda terrorists attacked America on September 11, 2001, if you had engaged the full power of the US military to take out al Qaeda and bin Laden, they would no longer have been a threat to any country—not to the United States, and certainly not to Iraq. Anybody in America with a clear perspective knows you railroaded your country into an unnecessary war. Senator Ted Kennedy said, 'Bush's distortions misled Congress into its war vote. No president of the United States should employ distortion of the truth to take the nation to war.' A *New York Times* editorial two years into your war stated, 'The president did not allow the American people, or even Congress, to have the information necessary to make reasoned judgments of their own.' A *New York Times*/CBS nationwide poll taken after your war showed that the majority of Americans believed you intentionally misled the nation to promote war.

"What you did, George W. Bush, is universally unpopular, but the question before the Court now is whether or not it was criminal. Do the crimes you personally committed constitute war crimes, as defined by international law? In this arena, these three judges will have to make the decision. But the majority of people around the world think they do."

Former president Bush was visibly upset. He looked away in anger, took a moment to compose himself, and shot back.

"It's not a criminal act for a president to do what he was elected to do by the American people."

"Oh, really? The American people elected you to send their sons and daughters to the other side of the world, and spend their treasury, to fight a needless, reckless, and illegal war?"

The entire proceeding came to a standstill. Perhaps figuring he might have said something he shouldn't have, Bush changed the subject.

"I might add that for the seven remaining years I was president after the 9/11 attacks, there were no other terrorist attacks on the United States. You can find plenty of Americans who would say that stopping terrorist attacks was worth it, at whatever the cost. I made America a safer place, period."

"I'd like to call the Court's attention to a curious series of events," McBride said, seemingly reignited by Bush's comment. "The last act of Bill Clinton's presidency was to sign a document that would've paved the way for the United States to become a member of the ICC. One of your first acts as president was to 'unsign' that agreement, effectively eliminating any chance of the United States joining the ICC. You obviously did that because you suspected you would be engaging in acts during your presidency that would violate international laws, and you didn't want to be subject to ICC jurisdiction."

White had heard enough. "Objection, Your Honors. Attempting to prejudice the judges' opinion."

Hurst-Brown agreed. "Objection sustained."

"Ironically, Mr. Bush, you would be the last person to quarrel with the death penalty," Michael McBride continued, all but ignoring the ruling. "As governor of Texas, you were a strong proponent of the death penalty. In fact, you had the highest execution rate of any governor in American history. You signed death warrants for all but one of one hundred and fifty-three prisoners."

Ed White pushed back again. "Objection! Irrelevant to this case!"

Hurst-Brown agreed. "Objection sustained."

McBride moved on. "There is no reason, legal or otherwise, why you, George W. Bush, should not be found guilty for the war crimes of which you are accused. We all know that no one is above the law. I trust you agree that includes presidents of the United States?"

For the first time, Bush agreed with McBride. "Correct, no man is above the law. But there's man's law and there's God's law."

McBride smiled faintly, as though he had been given the opening he had been waiting for. "What does God say to you about killing hundreds of thousands of people?"

"What God says to me is none of your business."

"'Thou shalt not kill,' and 'Love thy neighbor;' aren't those two of the most important commandments?"

"This is ridiculous. That was war," Bush protested.

"Did God personally tell you to go to war?"

"Objection!" White interrupted, trying to protect his client. "Badgering the witness."

Hurst-Brown disagreed. "Objection overruled."

"Before you were president, you delivered a sermon in church," McBride said, increasing in intensity. "Wearing a robe and standing in front of a choir, you said, 'I have a sense of calm knowing that the Bible's admonition, "Thy will be done," is life's guide.'"

"I was in church, quoting scripture," Bush responded indignantly and added, "If you don't believe in the word of the Lord, that's your problem."

"But isn't this a question of separation of church and state?" McBride asked rhetorically. "When America's Founding Fathers were creating the Declaration of Independence, Thomas Jefferson wrote the first draft. He originally wrote, 'We hold these truths to be *sacred*, that all men are created equal.' After completing his first draft, Jefferson gave it to Benjamin Franklin and asked for comments. Franklin rewrote the sentence to read, 'We hold these truths to be *self-evident*, that all men are created equal.' Benjamin Franklin was urging the Founding Fathers to create a nation in which democracy comes from reason, not religion—to make America's values the common sense of well-meaning people, not ordained by God."

"I've had about all his bullshit I can take," Bush said, looking over at his attorneys. "Do I have to take any more of this from him?"

Without waiting for an answer and much to the surprise of everyone in the courtroom, Bush stood up and headed toward the door. White stood to protest as well.

"The prosecution has made a mockery of this case," White said. "It's disrespectful and abusive to President Bush, and disgusting and demeaning to all of us involved."

With that, the defense attorneys quickly gathered their papers and followed Bush toward the exit.

"Order in the Court. Order in the Court," Hurst-Brown declared and rapped his gavel.

Bush was blocked at the door by two ICC security guards, and other guards contained his defense team. It created a standoff of sorts: George Bush and his defense team versus the ICC guards.

"Mr. Bush," Hurst-Brown admonished, "you and your defense team need to go back to your respective seats and sit down. The Court will deal with this matter, but you need to sit down first before anything else will happen."

Bush and his defense team exchanged looks and, presumably figuring they couldn't get past the ICC guards and out the door, returned to their seats. Once they were seated, Hurst-Brown turned to McBride.

"Mr. McBride, do you have any further questions?"

"Yes, Your Honor, we do."

"Then you may continue."

"Thank you, Your Honor," McBride said, turning back to Bush to continue his barrage. "Nine months into your war, no WMD had been found, Baghdad had fallen, and Saddam had been captured. Did you ever consider stopping your war at that time?

Bush seemed agitated and defensive. "Our goal was not just to get Saddam Hussein. Our goal was to bring freedom and democracy to Iraq, as I said before."

"The people of Iraq didn't want or need your democracy," McBride shot back. "Since the beginning of recorded history, countries around the world have had various forms of governments: fascism, totalitarianism, communism, dictatorships, democracies. The citizens of a country should be free to follow whatever form of government they so choose. Some countries do not want and cannot support a democracy, whether the United States likes it or not. The Vietnam War, like your war, was a terrible war fought at a monumental cost of lives and money. And yet Vietnam never was going to be anything else but a communist country. The United States should have no say in how other sovereign countries wish to rule themselves. How would you like it if Russia or China invaded the United States and tried to dictate its form of government?"

Bush's response dripped with disdain. "That's an absurd question, McBride, and you know it."

McBride didn't take the bait and moved on. "Your war converted an Iraq that was virtually free of terrorists at that time into a safe haven for new militant extremist groups to form and grow. And as if all that isn't bad enough, your war angered and alienated the entire Muslim world."

"The nature of history is that people understand the full consequences of actions only in the future, but inaction has consequences as well. Imagine what the world would be today with Saddam Hussein still ruling Iraq. He would be threatening his neighbors, sponsoring terror cells, and piling bodies into mass graves. The rising price of oil would have yielded him great wealth and power, and the American people would be much less secure. Instead, as a result of our actions, one of America's most dangerous enemies stopped threatening us forever. Hostile nations around the world saw clearly the cost of supporting terror and pursuing WMD. Millions of Iraqis went from living under a dictatorship of fear to having the prospects of a peaceful, functioning democracy."

"George W. Bush, not surprisingly, you and I have different views of what military strength should be about," McBride countered. "I definitely think America should have a strong military to protect and defend its people and their allies, not to attack and conquer, as America tried to do in Vietnam and Iraq."

"We weren't trying to conquer anybody," Bush protested. "We were trying to create a democracy where people could vote for their leaders and not live under the oppression of a ruthless and heartless tyrant. You have this wild-eyed compulsion to rewrite history."

Ignoring the insult, McBride pushed forward. "Early on in the war, you banned the American press from showing caskets of dead American soldiers when they returned home and from publicizing the growing number of American soldiers killed in your war. Why did you do that?"

Bush didn't answer.

"Was it because you didn't want the American people to realize you were exploiting their patriotism by putting their sons and daughters in harm's way for no good reason? Or was it because if they knew the truth about your war, there would've been anarchy in the streets, as there was during the Vietnam War? Huge public protests would likely have occurred all across the nation, and ultimately the American people would have demanded a stop to your war. And then, just maybe, you would've been impeached."

Bush looked over at White, apparently expecting him to object. Before White could say anything, however, McBride added, "Yes, impeached. Then after you were disgracefully removed from office, you could've been tried in an American court for murder, like you are finally being tried in this Court."

"Objection!" White interjected. "Baiting the witness."

"Objection sustained."

Bush answered, anyway. "Presidents Roosevelt, Truman, Johnson, Nixon, Clinton, and my father waged wars and were not impeached."

"But why should American presidents get away with mass murder and other crimes if they wage a war against another country on the other side of the world that is not legally justifiable under international law?"

"You've got to get real, McBride. In the real world, those charged with governing sovereign nations have to make unimaginably tough judgments—real-time, live, immensely complicated judgments about war and peace. And most do so with the best interests of their people at heart."

"Okay. Let's talk about the 'best interests' of people. We know the approximate number of lives lost in your war: one million, about four thousand five hundred of which were American soldiers, with the rest being coalition soldiers and Iraqi citizens. The number wounded physically and/or mentally is in the hundreds of thousands. Less important but equally notable is the monetary cost of your war: four trillion dollars and counting. For those of us who do not know, a trillion has twelve zeros; it takes about ten seconds to write down. If you want to talk about the best interests of your people, think about all the good the money spent on your war could've done fighting poverty, illiteracy, hunger, climate change, crumbling infrastructure, and the list goes on."

Bush snapped back. "None of that would matter if America couldn't defend herself against her enemies."

"Mr. Bush, try to see this for what it is. After 9/11, there was a tremendous outpouring of concern and sympathy from around the world for America. America's forefathers had built a country that represented hope and promise, freedom and opportunity, charity and compassion. But your war ruptured and reversed the world's opinion of the United States."

Bush shook his head slowly. "You're trying to portray me as a vicious and evil man. I am not."

Bush paused to collect himself. Everyone in the courtroom, public gallery, and around the world waited anxiously to hear what former President Bush would say next. Finally, with a hint of sadness, he continued.

"The Iraq War was emotional for me. I prayed for the strength to do the Lord's will. I'm not trying to justify war based on God, but I prayed that I would be a good messenger of His will. I prayed for forgiveness."

McBride responded with a rare hint of compassion. "Once, when you took part in a presidential debate in St. Louis, a lady asked you to comment on the mistakes you made. Remember what you said?"

"When people ask about mistakes, they're trying to say, 'Did you make a mistake going into Iraq?' The answer is absolutely not. It was the right decision. I'm fully prepared to accept any mistakes that history judges to my administration, because the president makes the decisions. The president has to take the responsibility."

"Yes. Finally, something we agree on. The president makes the decisions. The president has to take the responsibility." McBride turned to the judges. "No further questions at this time, Your Honors. The prosecution rests."

Judge Hurst-Brown announced a recess and gaveled the session over.

No doubt following the grueling prosecution questioning of former President Bush, all participants in the case had had a fitful night's sleep, with the possible exception of the judges.

George W. Bush's daily schedule complied with strict regulations mandated for all prisoners. Up at 6:30 AM (at which time he would say his morning prayers), breakfast at seven, exercise, shave, shower, and dress (today, white button-down shirt, blue sweater, gray slacks). At 8:30 AM sharp, he was loaded into an armored vehicle that pulled away under heavy protection. As soon as the military caravan turned right to leave the detention compound, the ICC building could be seen two and a half kilometers down a perfectly straight road.

By 9:00 AM, everyone had assembled and taken their usual places and the Court's day began.

"Mr. White, would defense like to redirect questioning of this witness?"

"Yes, Your Honor, we most certainly would."

"Then you may proceed."

"Thank you, Your Honor." White stood and drifted toward his longtime friend. "In the end, Mr. President, as we all know, war is tragic. A head of state has a seemingly endless number of tough decisions to make. He or she must do what they believe is right for the protection of their people and preservation of the common good. Mr. Bush, as you look back now, what thoughts do you have about that war?"

Bush seemed weary but pleased to answer the question. "Over the years, I've spent a great deal of time thinking about what went wrong in Iraq. I have concluded that we made two errors. The first is that in the ten months following the invasion, I cut troop levels from one hundred and ninety-two thousand to one hundred and nine thousand. That was a mistake. The second was the intelligence failure regarding weapons of mass destruction. I believed that the intelligence on Iraq's WMD was solid. If Saddam didn't have WMD, why wouldn't he just prove it to the inspectors? Obviously, he never thought the United States would follow through on its promises to disarm him by force. If America is going to continue to be the leader of the free world, it must stand up to its obligations, as difficult and controversial as they may be."

"Mr. Bush," White continued, "isn't it true that the entire executive branch of the United States government, including Vice President Dick Cheney, Secretary of Defense Don Rumsfeld, Secretary of State Colin Powell, National Security Advisor Condoleezza Rice, and others aggressively petitioned Congress to sanction the Iraq War?"

"Yes."

"And did you understand that the majority vote of the US Senate, including 'yea' votes from senators Hillary Clinton and John Kerry, and the majority of the House of Representatives, provided clear and irrefutable approval of the Iraq War?"

"Yes."

"And such approval was near unanimously supported by the American people?"

"Yes."

"And following the overwhelming support of the United States Congress and the American people, the United Nations passed Resolution 1441, which demanded that Iraq comply with long-standing UN mandates, or there would be 'serious consequences'?"

"Yes."

"And did you and others in your administration take 'serious consequences' to mean war, if necessary?"

"Yes."

"So in the months and weeks leading up to the Iraq War, you understood that you had the consent and approval of the US Congress, the American people, and the United Nations to wage war on Iraq and its ruthless dictator, Saddam Hussein?"

"Yes."

Believing he had successfully executed an important question-and-answer session with his client, White turned and said simply to the judges, "Thank you, Your Honors. May the strict application of the law be your guide. No further questions."

McBride seized the moment.

"Your Honors, the prosecution requests permission to re-cross."

"Permission granted."

"Thank you. Your Honors, first let's set the record straight. The US Congress and UN Security Council authorizations do not provide legal defense against the prosecution of George Bush for war crimes. Congress only provided the authorization for Mr. Bush to 'protect and defend' America—not fight a war on the other side of the world against an enemy he did not have. And UN Resolution 1441 was only a relisting of complaints regarding Iraq's lack of compliance with past mandates, and did not specifically authorize the use of force. George Bush, and his friend in England, Tony Blair, had no legal authority to wage their war against Iraq, and thus it is in breach of international law. Former Prime Minister Tony Blair's complicity in these crimes will be the subject of future investigation and trial."

McBride turned to address the former president, who looked ten years older than he had upon his arrival at The Hague a month earlier.

"Mr. Bush, your father was smart enough to leave Saddam alive and in power. You were not. Your disastrous war disrupted and disrespected the Muslim people and their religion. And now the rest of the world, including Christians, Jews, atheists, and others, are paying the price. Nobody won in your war, Mr. Bush. Everybody on all sides lost. Do you have anything else to say?"

Not only were the eyes of everyone in the courtroom focused on Bush, but also those of everyone in the public gallery (including Laura), the thousands outside watching the huge video monitors, and the millions more in public areas of cities large and small around the world. The total viewership during this phase of the trial was estimated to be one billion people, approximately one-tenth of the world's population.

Finally, Bush looked McBride directly in the eye and said, "No. Nothing I haven't already said."

"Okay. I have one last thing to ask. After the war, your ally Tony Blair admitted he was wrong and apologized. There is something noble about a man who is brave enough to admit he was wrong, regardless of how painful it might be. Here's your chance. Would you like to make an apology?"

After considering the question for a long moment, Bush answered.

"No apology necessary. After the attacks of 9/11, I did what needed to be done to protect and defend the American people and to rebuild my nation's trust in its government. I made America a safer place. That's what I was charged to do, and that's what I did. I make no apologies for it. I am sorry for the loss of life on both sides, but, as history has proven, there is a great price to pay for freedom. I have a clear conscience about what I did. I am an American citizen first, and a citizen of the world second. Whatever this Court decides will never change my love for, and allegiance to, the United States of America."

"Mr. Bush, every human being is a citizen of the world, whether they like it or not," McBride said, refusing to leave it at that. "Just as you are a citizen of Texas, you are a citizen of the United States, and just as you are a citizen of the United States, you are a citizen of the world. And if you commit crimes of international consequence, you will be held accountable by the International Criminal Court, like everybody else in the world."

McBride stared at Bush, who stared back and said nothing. Finally, McBride turned to the judges.

"No further questions, Your Honors."

Hurst-Brown announced the case would be in recess until further notice and rapped his gavel. The clerk announced, "All rise," and all did. The ICC judges stood and quickly made their exit.

11

Final Arguments

*"The wrongs we seek to condemn and punish have
been so calculated, so malignant, and so devastating
that civilization cannot tolerate their being ignored,
because it cannot survive their being repeated."*
—ROBERT H. JACKSON, CHIEF UNITED STATES PROSECUTOR
AT THE NUREMBERG TRIALS

IN TRUTH, THE IRAQ WAR HADN'T BEEN MUCH OF A WAR. Baghdad
had fallen within weeks. For all intents and purposes, that had
signaled the end of the war. The country that was Iraq before
the war had been vanquished. Not only would the war eventually
kill nearly a million people, two million more would be displaced
from their homes. The newly formed Iraqi government would
never be considered anything more than a puppet regime of the
United States, and over time it would begin to unravel. George
W. Bush's war had destroyed the country of Iraq, at least for the
foreseeable future.

Following the war, most reputable Iraqis had sought to per-
petuate the Muslim way of life, find their own collective identity
absent a ruthless dictator or foreign invaders, and hold accountable
those who were responsible for the war. It was this mindset that
had led a group of patriotic Iraqis to petition the ICC to bring
George W. Bush to trial for war crimes.

With the ravages of his war still very much in evidence, it was understandable that George Bush's trial would receive extensive coverage in Iraq. One of the news agencies covering the trial was the web-based *Aswat al-Iraq*, which translated means "voices of Iraq." Aswat's writer, Bishara Nassim, had studied history and law in both France and the United States, and wrote the following after the conclusion of Bush's testimony:

"It is evident that George W. Bush is being tried at the ICC under the well-established guidelines of international criminal law, and has had the benefit of the defense counsel of his own choosing. In contrast to Bush's trial, let's look at the trial of Saddam Hussein. In December 2003, nine months into the war, US soldiers captured Hussein near his hometown of Tikrit. Most people who advocated for the protection of fundamental human rights and the just application of international law assumed an international criminal tribunal would try President Hussein. After all, such had been the case for other accused leaders such as Slobodan Milošević, Radovan Karadžić, and Joseph Kony.

"But no such thing happened. After being held captive for a year and a half, Hussein was brought to trial in what was known as the Iraqi High Tribunal and charged with the killing of one hundred and forty-eight Shiite Iraqis in retaliation for an assassination attempt on his life in 1982. He was not charged for any crimes against America or other countries in the coalition.

"Before the trial, Hussein's defense team requested a delay in the proceedings, insisting it had not been given all the evidentiary materials that had been secured by the prosecution, and did not have sufficient time to evaluate the evidence they had been given. The request was denied.

"In his first trial appearance, Hussein vigorously rejected the tribunal's legitimacy and its independence from America's control, stating, 'I do not respond to this so-called Court, and I retain my constitutional rights as the president of Iraq. Neither do I recognize the government that has designated and authorized you.'

"On November 5, 2006, Hussein was found guilty and sentenced to death by hanging. On December 30, 2006, at an Iraqi army base in Baghdad known as Camp Justice, Saddam Hussein, without having been provided the due process of law, which is mandated for all human beings regardless of the severity of crime or crimes in question, was hung.

"There was much worldwide comment about the reaction to Hussein's death. In the United States, President George W. Bush stated, 'Saddam Hussein's trial is a milestone in the Iraqi people's efforts to replace the rule of a tyrant with the rule of law.' In Rome at the Vatican, Cardinal Martino said, 'For me, punishing a crime with another crime, which is what killing for vindication is, means that we are still at the point of demanding an eye for an eye, a tooth for a tooth.'"

On the morning following the publication of Nassim's article, a packed courtroom watched in silence as the ICC judges solemnly entered and marched to their chairs. What was at stake was abundantly clear: A guilty verdict would mean a former president of the United States could spend the rest of his life in prison, while an innocent verdict would send Bush home and leave in question the very real possibility of more wars in the future and the viability of the ICC.

As usual, Judge Hurst-Brown gaveled the day to begin and called upon the prosecuting attorneys to make their final argument. Michael McBride, no doubt intending to stick the proverbial dagger into George Bush's heart, stood erect and addressed the Court in a clear and solemn voice.

"Your Honors, the implications of this trial have great historical significance. No one can deny the gravity of bringing a former president of the United States to the International Criminal Court to stand trial for war crimes. But in finality, you three judges are called upon to do what you have sworn to do, which is to apply the law as it relates to the conduct of humankind. A bedrock principle of justice holds that every man is equal before the law—pauper or president, president or pauper. As this Court has noted, no one, including leaders of superpowers, has impunity for acts he or she undertook while in office. Furthermore, war crimes can never be considered official acts of a sovereign state, and such crimes carry no statute of limitations. Mr. Bush cannot hide from his crimes, and he cannot hide from this Court. He is liable for his crimes just like anybody else, and remains so until the day he dies.

"Both documentary evidence and witness testimony have proven that the man seated before you today, George W. Bush, is guilty of both crimes against humanity and war crimes. He knowingly lied to the American people and the United States Congress, the approval of which was secured based on false accusations made by the defendant. And without valid approvals from the US Congress and the UN, Mr. Bush's presidential order to wage war was illegal, making his war a criminal act. During testimony, he revealed his intent to pursue a war that was illegal under international law, and with blatant disregard for the inevitable death of human beings, prisoner abuse, and massive destruction of property he certainly knew would result from his war.

"Article 25(3) of the Rome Statute states, 'a person shall be criminally responsible and liable for punishment for a crime within the jurisdiction of the Court if that person: a) commits such a crime, whether as an individual, jointly with another or through another person, regardless of whether that other person is criminally responsible; b) orders, solicits or induces the commission of such a crime which in fact occurs or is attempted; c) for the purpose of facilitating the commission of such a crime, aids, abets or otherwise assists in its commission or its attempted commission, including providing the means for its commission; d) in any other way contributes to the commission or the attempted commission of such a crime by a group of persons acting with a common purpose.'"

McBride turned to the judges and pleaded with all his might. "Your Honors, the prosecution has proven beyond any reasonable doubt that George Bush is guilty of each and every one of these acts—a, b, c, and d, as stated—and must be found guilty. As president of the United States, not only was he the chief executive officer, but also the constitutionally mandated commander in chief. As such, he was in charge of all armed forces at the disposal of the US government.

"Under the command responsibility doctrine, as the chain of command in the United States ends with the president, the president must be and is the person most responsible for the commission of crimes. Through this well-established legal concept, the perpetrator need not have pulled the trigger to commit the crime. Courts have long held that a commander who orders his subordinates to act unlawfully bears full responsibility for the actions that follow from his orders.

"Additionally, we urge the Court to find George W. Bush guilty of crimes under the legal doctrine of joint criminal enterprise. In a war such as the Iraq War, soldiers are considered merely innocents doing their duty as ordered by their commander. The commander is criminally liable, as he had the duty to know and identify civilian versus combatant targets in the field of battle.

"Next, with respect to derivative liability, we urge you to find the defendant guilty of war crimes under Article (25)(3)(c), which includes the concept of aiding and abetting. Under this form of liability, George W. Bush aided and abetted by virtue of the fact he secured congressional approval and ordered the US military into action, which inexorably led to the commission of these crimes. Your Honors, respectfully I remind the Court that aiding and abetting carries the same penalty as if one committed the crime or crimes oneself.

"George W. Bush ordered the invasion of Iraq in blatant disregard of international law and in reckless disdain for the terrible consequences that would certainly follow. He engaged an army that was underprepared to conduct postwar humanitarian operations and untrained in the proper handling of prisoners of war. Tragically, he empowered a military force with the most technologically advanced weaponry available to exact the maximum amount of death and destruction on an imagined enemy."

McBride paused to give the judges time to assimilate his assertions.

"Your Honors, the weight of this decision is great. With approximately five thousand American soldiers and more than six hundred fifty thousand Iraqi citizens dead as a result of George W. Bush's war, the implications of your decision will impact countless victims and their survivors. After the attacks of September 11, 2001, the great majority of the world's population would have understood America bringing to justice those who carried out the attacks: al Qaeda and Osama bin Laden. But for whatever incomprehensible reason, George Bush did not do that.

"Tragically, we all know the results of his war. Not only were al Qaeda and the Taliban not destroyed, but they also got stronger. Radical Muslims in the Middle East banded together to protect their religious rights and principles. The Islamic State took form, a faceless enemy without a geographical home, recruiting and training disenfranchised youths over the Internet to fight an unholy jihad, and all of it traced back to George W. Bush's war.

"In truth, America would have been better off if Mr. Bush had befriended Saddam Hussein, as President Reagan had done during the Iran-Iraq War, rather than destroyed him, because Saddam may have stopped the creation of ISIS before it started."

McBride glanced over to study the judges. He couldn't tell whether they were with him or not, so he continued with even more passion.

"Your Honors, the evidence is clear. Common sense makes it even more obvious. George W. Bush waged an illogical, illegal, and unnecessary war. Now you, the judges of the International Criminal Court, must determine his fate. In so doing, you may well be determining the destiny of humankind. Finding him innocent will doom our children and our children's children to a world of hate, fear, aggression, and more wars. Finding him guilty will send a clear message to all heads of state that they can no longer wage unnecessary and illegal wars against sovereign nations with impunity. In just this way, you may turn the tide of humanity away from its seemingly irresistible urge to fight military battles.

"Here and now, this Court represents the hopes and dreams of all peace-loving peoples of the world. What will it be: Love or hate? Peace or war? Survival or mutually assured destruction? Your Honors, you must each have the courage to discharge your duties under the oath you took when accepting your appointment as a judge in this Court to uphold the law. Simply put, the destiny of humankind could be at stake."

The judges sat motionless. McBride paused for a moment and then went for the big finish.

"In the name of justice, out of respect for the dignity of all humankind, in pursuit of swift and sure application of international law, in validation of what the International Criminal Court was intended to be, and in the precious quest for peace on Earth, we ask you, the esteemed judges of the ICC—no, the people of the world plead with you—to find George W. Bush guilty of one or more of the war crimes of which he is accused, and of which he is clearly guilty. Thank you, Your Honors. The prosecution rests."

"Thank you, Mr. McBride and Ms. Shadid," Judge Hurst-Brown said with all due solemnity. "Defense may proceed with final arguments."

Ed White glanced at his friend sitting alone and vulnerable in the accused's box. Bush gave him a thumbs-up and smiled a half-hearted smile. White nodded, cleared his throat, and began.

"Thank you, Your Honors. In World War II, free nations came together to fight the ideologies of fascism and imperialism—Adolf Hitler in Germany, Hideki Tojo in Japan, Benito Mussolini in Italy—and freedom prevailed. Today, Germany, Japan, and Italy are vibrant democracies and much-trusted members of the international community of sovereign nations. Who is to say the young democracy that is trying to survive in Iraq will not in time be the very thing that ultimately transitions Iraq from an isolated rogue nation to a thriving country recognized as a member in good standing by friendly countries around the world?

"The results of war are often not understood until years after the final shots are fired. The prosecution's contention is that what happened in Iraq was an international armed conflict. It was not. It was a strategic mission by the United States and its allies to specifically remove a known terrorist from power. No one could dispute that Saddam Hussein had been a threat to the United States and had waged various forms of warfare against her allies, including Israel and Kuwait. Given Saddam Hussein's violent temper and aggressive conduct over decades, and given the availability of more sophisticated and mobile weaponry in the chaos following the 9/11 attacks, he clearly posed an immediate and direct threat to the United States.

"Moreover, strictly speaking in legal terms, Mr. Bush could not be guilty of crimes during the Iraq War for the simple reason that Congress passed a joint resolution authorizing him to use the Armed Forces of the United States as he determined to be necessary in order to defend America. I emphasize *as he determined to be necessary,* not how the prosecution or, with all due respect, even the judges here at the ICC determine. To underscore the enthusiasm Congress had for the Iraq War, after Mr. Bush's speech, the assemblage rose up in unison and gave him a two-minute standing ovation.

"Furthermore, the United Nations Security Council had unanimously passed a joint resolution admonishing Iraq for past non-compliance with regard to weapons inspections and mandated new inspections. How can anyone treat Mr. Bush like a criminal for doing the very thing he was elected to do by the American people, and authorized to do by both the United States Congress and the United Nations?"

White directly addressed the judges to deliver what he believed would be a knockout blow. "Your Honors, at this time I would like to introduce US Attorney General Thomas K. Harding and, with permission of the Court, yield the floor to him so he can deliver a message from the current president of the United States."

The entire courtroom reacted with surprise as Attorney General Harding, dressed in a conservative dark gray suit and emitting an air of imperious confidence, entered the courtroom and headed toward the defense table. ICC judges conferred. Prosecuting attorneys sensed trouble and debated what, if anything, they could do. Defense attorneys welcomed their comrade.

The hubbub in the courtroom was silenced when Hurst-Brown rapped his gavel and stated, "The Court recognizes US Attorney

General Thomas Harding and welcomes him. Mr. Harding, would you please read the swearing-in document?"

Nadia Shadid stood to protest. "Objection, Your Honors. This highly irregular stunt the defense is attempting violates well-established legal doctrines and protocol. The prosecution requests a recess in order to properly frame a response, and to prepare for cross-examination, should it be needed."

Hurst-Brown responded immediately. "Thank you, Ms. Shadid. The prosecution's objection is noted, but denied. The defense has only asked permission for the attorney general to submit a request to the Court. No interactive questioning will occur and no testimony given. Objection overruled."

Reluctantly, Shadid sat. Attorney General Harding nodded confidently at the judges and read the swearing-in document.

"Thank you, sir. You may proceed," Judge Hurst-Brown responded.

"Thank you, Your Honors," Harding replied and began his statement. "First, I would like to apologize to the Court for my abrupt and irregular entrance. I appear before you as an official emissary of both the president of the United States and the United States Department of Justice. We consider the abduction of former President George W. Bush by the ICC to be in blatant violation of international laws, and hold all those who participated in these illegal acts responsible in criminal courts in the United States in due course. Furthermore, we categorically reject the ICC's contention that it had the necessary legal authority to transfer former President Bush here to The Hague and force him to stand trial in this Court. It is worth noting that the United States, as a member of the United Nations and specifically a permanent member of the Security Council, was party to the ratification of the ICC, and from the beginning has worked to support many of the organizational and procedural needs of the ICC.

"However, along with registering the considerable repugnance and objection of the American people for the illegal and disrespectful treatment of a former president, I come with a proposal. As you must know, one of the original tenets of international law is the important principle of admissibility, as defined by the complementarity rule. For those unaware, Article 17 of the Rome Statute provides that the ICC shall consider a case admissible only when the home state of the alleged perpetrator, in this case the United States of America, is 'unwilling or unable to genuinely carry out the investigation.' This important doctrine of the ICC charter is meant to protect against and specifically disallow unnecessary prosecution, such as this.

"Speaking on behalf of the president of the United States and the US Department of Justice, I hereby inform the ICC that the United States invokes this complementarity rule and requests Mr. Bush's immediate release so that he can be returned to his home country to be tried for the alleged offenses of which he has been accused by this chamber."

Pandemonium broke out both inside and outside the Court. Judge Hurst-Brown repeatedly pounded his gavel and called for order. Eventually, the courtroom fell silent and Harding calmly continued his statement.

"We do not wish to disrupt or invalidate the ICC. Nor do we wish to bring military action against the ICC. We simply request that the ICC immediately discharge Mr. Bush and turn him over to the custody of the United States, in which case he will be transported back to the United States to stand trial. We have a fleet of US military jets standing by, and I will personally escort him home."

Shadid stood to interrupt. "Your Honors, prosecution requests the opportunity to respond."

"First," Hurst-Brown replied, "the Court would like to ask the attorney general if he has anything else to say."

"No, sir. Our request is simple, and we expect the ICC to look upon it favorably."

"Is it the intention of the United States to put Mr. Bush on trial in the near future?" Hurst-Brown said, sounding slightly skeptical.

"Meaning?"

"Meaning as soon as would be practical," Hurst-Brown snapped back.

"How would you define that, sir?" Harding responded, side-stepping the question.

"Within the next few months, less than a year."

If this were a chess game, the attorney general would have been put in check by the ICC judge. Knowing that if he wanted to get the answer he needed, he had to give the judges a response they would accept, Harding said, "Fair enough, Your Honors. The United States will endeavor to commence the trial within twelve months of Mr. Bush's release from this court."

"Endeavor to commence, or commit to commence?"

Attorney General Harding considered the implications of his answer carefully before answering.

"The United States will commit to commence the trial within twelve months of Mr. Bush's release."

"Thank you, Mr. Harding," Hurst-Brown said, turning to Nadia. "Ms. Shadid, does the prosecution wish to address the Court on this matter?"

"Yes, Your Honor, we do," she said, standing.

"Please proceed."

"Respectfully, Your Honors, this request by the United States cannot and must not be granted. The Iraq War was over in December 2011, and under any fair assessment the United States has had more than enough time to bring charges against George W. Bush. Moreover, Article 17 of the Rome Statute provides that when there has been an unjustified delay in the proceedings demonstrating an unwillingness or inability to prosecute, the jurisdiction of the case transfers to the ICC. As the Iraq War ended in 2011, the United States has had ample time to prosecute this case and must be deemed to have defaulted on its obligation. The people of Iraq and the United States, indeed all the peoples of the world deserve to have this case adjudicated upon by the most universally accepted of all courts, the International Criminal Court."

"Thank you, Ms. Shadid," Hurst-Brown stated, "your concerns are duly noted."

With three more well-struck blows of his gavel, Hurst-Brown declared the Court adjourned, bringing an end to a notably important and unprecedented day in the life of the International Criminal Court.

12

Can There Be Justice?

*"If there is not justice for the high and mighty like
justice for the common man, then there is no justice."*

—Anonymous

THE EVENTS IN THE HAGUE SET OFF A TSUNAMI of international press reports that ricocheted around the world. While the world's international law experts had provided volumes of commentary on what might or might not happen in the case against George W. Bush, none of them had imagined this. Legal eagles, politicians, law students, military personnel, and news junkies had followed and debated the case nonstop, while others had been content to catch snippets on the evening news. In both the USA and the UK, as public opinion was divided nearly equally, news reporting needed to be especially balanced, so as to not advocate for one side or the other and thus anger half the audience.

Following US Attorney General Harding's appearance at the ICC, the BBC's Elizabeth Reynolds invited renowned British solicitor Sir Nigel Pemberton back to her broadcast to provide clarity and perspective.

"For those who are not legal junkies, the complementarity rule simply means that all nations, including those that are not members of the ICC, have the responsibility to either prosecute suspected perpetrators of international crimes, or extradite them to the ICC for trial," Pemberton said. "In fact, in international criminal law, the only way the ICC can try a case is if a nation is unable or unwilling to genuinely prosecute the matter in question. The principle here is that national governments have the first right to prosecute if they so choose."

Reynolds pressed Pemberton for clarification. "And if they cannot or do not wish to prosecute, the International Criminal Court becomes the next option, correct?" she asked.

"Correct, but the United States is invoking the complementarity rule now, even though the Iraq War ended more than a decade ago."

"Is there a statute of limitation in international law in relation to such matters? In other words, how long can a country can procrastinate in connection with a prosecution?" Reynolds asked, seeking to address the obvious questions.

"In international law, the complementarity rule is silent on the question of time. In fact, this case before us now may well provide legal precedent for this matter in the future."

"Interesting," Reynolds commented, raising her eyebrows. "The question then becomes: What would such a ruling do to the credibility of the ICC?"

"Yes, it's a judgment call. Or they may elect to invoke the spirit of the Rome Statute, so to speak, which allows for the country in which the accused lives to have the first crack at a case, irrespective of time, thus allowing the Americans to prosecute Mr. Bush as they are pledging to do."

"And so, Sir Nigel, the question becomes what would such a ruling do to the credibility of the ICC?"

"From the perspective of the international legal community, the ICC has demonstrated with this case that it means business. The fact that it brought the Bush case to trial in the first place is a significant validation, not only of its legitimacy, but also for its longevity. Early on in the proceeding, the judges countered very difficult legal challenges and succeeded nobly in demonstrating the ICC's capacity to hear the case. Indeed, if the ICC does decide to step aside in favor of the complementarity rule and let the United States prosecute the case, it might even be applauded for its deference to the sovereignty of individual countries, thereby refuting many of the remaining arguments against the ICC, especially from Republicans in the US Senate."

Reynolds pressed for more. "What might happen if the ICC were to deny this request from the United States?"

"Well, the question then would be: If George W. Bush is found guilty at the ICC, how and when would Americans respond, and what would its military do, if anything?"

"It would be a fool's errand to speculate."

"Yes. All bets would be off the table."

"High drama indeed at the International Criminal Court," Reynolds concluded with a hint of intrigue. "Stay tuned for continuing coverage."

All principal *dramatis personae* assembled in the courtroom on the following morning, including US Attorney General Thomas Harding. Presiding Judge Hurst-Brown gaveled and announced the Court back in session and came right to the point with breathtaking abruptness.

"Regarding the unprecedented request registered on behalf of former President George W. Bush and the US State Department, the Court has reached a decision . . . a unanimous one, I might add."

McBride and Shadid exchanged looks, as years of work done would come down to what was said in the next few seconds.

"The principle of complementarity was an important concept in the initial formation of international criminal law," Hurst-Brown continued. "In fact, it was debated, conceived, and drafted at the time by the greatest legal minds in the world. It was of unanimous consent that the country in which the perpetrator of a crime is domiciled has the first rights of prosecution, deliberation, and decision with regard to guilt or innocence. In fact, when considering future implications, the ICC would cease to fulfill its mandated purpose if it breached this fundamental concept in law. While there are questions about the length of time it has taken to exercise its right to first prosecution, the United States' fundamental rights relative to the complementarity rule remain in force."

Rapping his gavel three times, Hurst-Brown took a deep breath and issued the much-anticipated ruling.

"In the case of The Prosecutor v. George W. Bush, this Court yields to the request of the United States and agrees to release Mr. Bush into the custody of its officials with the understanding they will transport him back to the United States to stand trial within a period of twelve months from this date for crimes he is alleged to have committed in connection with the Iraq War."

Pandemonium erupted. Those in the public gallery and elsewhere who advocated for Bush's innocence cheered and hugged each other with joy and relief. Those who wanted George W. Bush to be found guilty responded with loud and indignant outrage. Inside the courtroom, the defense team was alternately hugging Bush and shaking Attorney General Harding's hand. The prosecuting attorneys were equal parts outraged and crestfallen. Nadia Shadid rose to her feet.

"Your Honors, please! The prosecution pleads for the opportunity to respond."

Judge Hurst-Brown pounded his gavel again to regain order and be heard. "Permission granted," he said.

Shadid launched into her objections with shocking intensity.

"Your Honors, this Court has buckled under this highly irregular and suspiciously tardy pressure placed upon it by the United States. This rupture of justice more than a decade after crimes were committed sets a dangerous precedent. From now on, other countries will simply monitor proceedings at the ICC, and if they're not comfortable with a likely outcome, invoke the complementarity rule, and the ICC will be forced by this precedent to yield. The inmates will be running the asylum. This will go down in history as a sad day in the life of the ICC specifically, and for international criminal law in general. I hope you understand the historical gravity of this decision, Your Honors, because you are all responsible for it."

"I caution you, Ms. Shadid," Hurst-Brown fired back. "You are moments away from being found in contempt and removed from this Court."

Nadia held her fire.

Hurst-Brown paused until order was restored. "Ms. Shadid, judges here at the ICC do not need a lecture, nor do they wish to be scolded," he said.

"Yes, Your Honor," Shadid acquiesced. "Please accept my apology."

Satisfied with Ms. Shadid's modest gesture of conciliation, Judge Hurst-Brown moved on.

"Apology accepted. Now, do you have anything else to say?"

"Yes, Your Honor. I yield to my colleague, Michael McBride.

"The Court recognizes Mr. McBride."

"Thank you, your Honor," McBride began. "For America to be the great nation it once was, it must take responsibility for the mistakes it has made. These mistakes most certainly include those made by George W. Bush in connection with the Iraq War. Mr. Bush, George, you waged your war with a coalition of military forces. If you are not found guilty, which I hope to God you are, how about you personally assembling a coalition of humanitarian forces to fix the mess you created in Iraq and the Middle East? Instead of fighting unnecessary wars, American politicians should be focusing their combined resources on solving problems that would elevate the human condition, problems such as climate change, hunger, illiteracy, poverty, illness, slavery, homelessness, child abuse, drug abuse, and so many others. How about we stop beating each other up and turn our collective attention to the very things that can make the human condition better, smarter, healthier, sane, safe, tolerant, more compassionate, and, yes, loving?"

McBride paused and wondered if anybody cared about what he had just said.

"We plead that at the very minimum this case will send a message to the citizens of the world, particularly to the youth, that they should not and must not go blindly into war just because their government tells them to, especially when it is, in actuality, such a tiny number of people that takes an entire country to war. Every human being should have a say about the conduct of his or her own life and the behavior of his or her own country, whether it contradicts the wishes of elected officials or not. That's what democracy is all about."

An awkward silence pervaded the courtroom before McBride, torn asunder by emotion, fired his final shot.

"The US government may have temporarily won this battle, but it has not won the war, the war that exists in the hearts and minds of the people of the world, the war between injustice and justice, cruelty and compassion, war and peace, hate and love."

Then, in a shocking act of defiance and disrespect, Michael McBride nodded at Nadia Shadid, and together they marched out of the courtroom. The onlookers sat stunned and silent. Nobody knew quite what to do or say. Finally, Judge Hurst-Brown rapped his gavel and said in a somber and somewhat weary voice, "The Prosecutor v. George W. Bush is closed, for the time being."

Ed White moved to former President Bush and hugged him triumphantly.

"Let's go home, George."

Bush took a deep breath and let it out.

"Yeah. I've had about all the fun here I can stand," Bush said, looking up at Laura in the gallery and signaling victory with a thumbs-up.

Laura returned the gesture and stood up to leave. Bush and his defense team quickly packed up their papers and headed for the exit. Veteran court observers sensed an awkward feeling of relief more than victory, knowing full well that this game was not over.

Off the coast in the North Sea, the USS *George H. W. Bush* swung around to a southerly heading and departed, destination unknown.

13

All Over
but the Shouting

*"The care of human life and happiness, and
not their destruction, is the first and only
legitimate object of good government."*
—THOMAS JEFFERSON

THERE IS SOMETHING DISAPPOINTING IF NOT INFURIATING about a story
without an ending. In theory, the United States had the moral obligation to live up to its pledge to put former President Bush on trial.
No one could be sure of that obligation being met, however.

Some judicial scholars were critical of the prosecution for not
winning a case that so many thought needed to be won for no less
a reason than the safety and security of all humankind. In the end,
the ICC got mostly high marks for bringing George W. Bush to
trial, and low marks for not rendering a final verdict.

There were many residual questions that only time would tell.
Would the United States put George W. Bush on trial? Would it
happen in the twelve months allotted? What would be the verdict?
If Bush were to be found innocent in American courts, would the
ICC be able to recapture him and bring him back to The Hague to
finish what it had started? If the case were to reconvene at the ICC,
would Michael McBride and Nadia Shadid serve as prosecuting

attorneys? If, in the future, other leaders of superpowers were to wage illegal wars, would the Bush trial have established enough precedent for the ICC to bring them to trial for their crimes? Would the ICC have secured its place as a legitimate international court to stand above all national courts, regardless of the implications of the case? Would the case of The Prosecutor v. George W. Bush have made the world a safer place or not?

On the morning after the trial, Michael McBride and Nadia Shadid met in the prosecution meeting room to collect their research books and trial documents. After many minutes of silence, which was rare for them, Nadia spoke.

"How are you doing?"

"I'm thinking about taking a long walk into the North Sea," Michael answered without smiling. "How about you?"

"I am every bit as hurt and disappointed as you are," she responded, disquieted by his frivolous attitude. "We didn't win the case, but we didn't lose it either. Not really."

"No good damning us with faint praise," he snapped back with a bit too much bite.

Growing slightly angry at his inappropriate behavior at a time like this, Nadia capitulated. They stared at each other for a long while before Michael, finally admiring her optimism in the wake of such disappointment, spoke again.

"I'm sorry, Nadia. You're right. Thank you for that. It means a lot to me, especially coming from you. I consider it to be an honor to have partnered with you."

Nadia smiled and decided to reciprocate the sentiment in the most Western way she could think of, offering an enthusiastic high five to her partner.

"The feeling is mutual, Michael. Next time, right?"

"Right."

Although Laura had brought George a suitcase full of clothes, for his own reasons he wanted to walk out of the ICC Detention Centre in the same clothes he had been wearing when he had walked in. As he finished putting on the golf clothes he had sported at St. Andrews, he took one last look around the prison cell that had been his home since that morning in September and walked out.

It was Mr. Bush's wish not to "sneak out of town," as he had put it, but rather to make the dignified exit of a confident man who knew all along he had done no wrong. Waiting in the foyer of the Detention Centre were Laura Bush, his three defense attorneys, six UN security guards, and a dozen armed US military personnel.

When George arrived in the foyer, he was greeted with a warm embrace from Laura, after which were handshakes and hugs with his defense team. Not much was said. They all knew too well that what had happened was not an ending but rather served to prompt questions about what was yet to come. Mr. Bush took Mrs. Bush's hand, and with more relief than triumph, they walked out of the Detention Centre.

There was no order in the assembled crowd outside. Some waved placards that read, "We Love You, President Bush," "Justice Is Served," and "Jesus Loves You, George." Other placards displayed the opposite sentiment: "George Bush, Murderer," "Hope You Burn in Hell," "Iraq's Blood Is on Your Hands." Standing side by side, some were yelling congratulations and well wishes while others were yelling protests, hatred, and threats.

During the brief walk to an awaiting helicopter, George Bush noticed a teenage girl waving an American flag. He smiled, nodded his approval, and flashed the "V" sign, a gesture that thrilled some and angered others.

Other than making sure no one got too close to the Bushes, the ICC security team simply moved them through the crowd and into the chopper. Not wanting any undue delay, the pilot had done his preflight check and, with the blades already whirling, lifted the chopper off to whisk George and Laura Bush away from the International Criminal Court and to a US military jet that would transport them back to America. As the chopper took off, the conflicted crowd availed themselves of the moment to yell their respectful goodbyes or angry invectives.

As the aircraft disappeared in the distance, people on the ground were left standing still and silent. Some wondered why others could not comprehend the horrible destruction of George W. Bush's war and the woeful miscarriage of justice that his escape from international law represented. Others wondered why some people could have so much hatred in their hearts that they couldn't grant love and forgiveness. Still others concluded that over time justice would be served, and that there was no need for apologies or forgiveness from anyone to anyone about anything.

Later that night, a very curious thing occurred. Michael McBride was nowhere to be found. He had agreed to meet Nadia in the prosecution offices to start packing up the mountain of evidence they had accumulated for the trial. But after working for an hour, Nadia realized Michael would not be coming. She tried his various phone numbers but had no luck. She went to a house he kept not far from the ICC, and even though the lights were on, he was not there.

First thing in the morning, Nadia called Michael's wife in London to inquire as to his whereabouts. Mrs. Stapleford-McBride said he had called to inform her about the resolution of the case, but other than that, she had not spoken to him at length in weeks, and rather dismissively suggested his sudden absence was how he always dealt with defeat.

Maybe she believes that, Nadia thought, *but not me.* The Michael McBride she knew would be a combination of heartbroken and pissed off about the outcome of a case they had worked on so hard for so long. At the end of her second day of searching, Nadia alerted ICC administrators, who in turn notified local police. Michael McBride, the highly respected and now internationally famous prosecuting attorney, was placed on a number of missing persons lists, first in Europe and then around the world, on which he would remain.

"Each night, when I go to sleep, I die.
And the next morning, when I wake up, I am reborn."
—Mahatma Gandhi

Bibliography

The activities of the president of the United States and other public figures have been well covered and documented by many news and information outlets. The actual statements made by the public figures referred to herein are a matter of public record, and thus available for public consumption and examination. Some quotes, of course, do not appear verbatim but rather were shaped to sound more like dialogue. I would like to acknowledge the mountain of material used in this novel that was written or spoken by others. In some ways, when it comes to this book, I was more of an aggregator of content than a writer, and as such, would like to acknowledge the many sources from which I drew that content.

Allawi, Ali A. *The Occupation of Iraq: Winning the War, Losing the Peace.* New Haven, CT: Yale University Press, 2007.

Blair, Tony. *A Journey: My Political Life.* New York, NY: Knopf, 2010.

Bush, George W. *Decision Points.* New York, NY: Crown, 2010.

Bush, Laura. *Spoken from the Heart.* New York, NY: Scribner, 2010.

Cheney, Dick. *In My Time.* New York, NY: Threshold Editions, 2011.

Clarke, Richard A. *Against All Enemies: Inside America's War on Terror.* New York, NY: Free Press, 2004.

Franks, Tommy. *American Soldier.* New York, NY: ReganBooks/HarperCollins, 2004.

Isikoff, Michael, and David Corn. *Hubris: The Inside Story of Spin, Scandal, and the Selling of the Iraq War.* New York, NY: Crown, 2006.

Kukis, Mark. *Voices from Iraq: A People's History, 2003–2009.* New York, NY: Columbia University Press, 2011.

Oborne, Peter. *Not the Chilcot Report.* London, UK: Head of Zeus, 2016.

Rice, Condoleezza. *No Higher Honor: A Memoir of My Years in Washington.* New York, NY: Crown, 2011.

Ricks, Thomas E. *Fiasco: The American Military Adventure in Iraq.* New York, NY: Penguin, 2006.

Riverbend. *Baghdad Burning: Girl Blog from Iraq.* New York, NY: The Feminist Press at CUNY, 2005.

Rumsfeld, Donald. *Known and Unknown: A Memoir.* New York, NY: Sentinel, 2011.

Schabas, William A. *An Introduction to the International Criminal Court.* Cambridge, UK: Cambridge University Press, 2017.

Woodward, Bob. *Plan of Attack.* New York, NY: Simon & Schuster, 2004.

Wright, Evan. *Generation Kill.* New York, NY: G. P. Putnam's Sons, 2004.

About the Author

Terry Jastrow received his bachelor's degree in communications from the University of Houston. Upon graduation, he worked for ABC Sports, where he became the youngest network producer/director in history. His credits include one Super Bowl, sixty-two major golf championships, and six Olympic games, including the opening and closing ceremonies of the 1984 Summer Olympics, which were watched by an estimated one billion people around the world. As a television producer/director, he has won seven Emmy Awards.

Terry Jastrow is also a published novelist, successful screenwriter, and noted playwright. His feature film work includes *Waltz Across Texas* (cowriter, producer, and star) and *The Squeeze* (writer, producer, and director). His stage work includes *The Trial of Jane Fonda* (writer and director) and *A Couple of White Chicks Sitting Around Talking* (director). In addition to *The Trial of George W. Bush,* he is also the author of the nonfiction title *Thought Is Boss.* He and his wife, Anne Archer, currently live in Los Angeles, California.